St.

Broad St.

Pelletier Ave.

Bacon St.

ne St.

Joe's Restaurant

ler St.

Elizabeth St.

Mary St

Bacon St.

St.

1303 Mary St.

Albany St.

Proctor Park

Starch Factory Creek

N.

W. E.

S.

Utica, New York

Albany Hill

The Music of the Inferno

SUNY series in
Italian/American Culture

Fred L. Gardaphe, editor

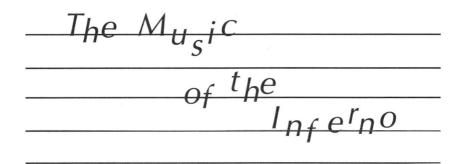

The Music of the Inferno

A Novel

by

FRANK LENTRICCHIA

Frank Lentricchia

STATE UNIVERSITY OF NEW YORK PRESS

Cover oil painting and interior ink sketches copyright © 1999 by Robert Cimbalo. Mr. Cimbalo teaches at Utica College.

Typeset in Utica by Partners Composition.
Covers printed in Utica by Brodock Press.

Production by Ruth Fisher
Marketing by Dana E. Yanulavich

Published by
State University of New York Press, Albany

For information, address the State University of New York Press, State University Plaza, Albany, NY 12246

Library of Congress Cataloging-in-Publication Data

Lentricchia, Frank.
  The music of the inferno / Frank Lentricchia.
    p.   cm.)
    ISBN 0-7914-4347-7 alk. paper. — ISBN 0-7914-4348-5 (pbk. : alk. paper
    1. Italian Americans—New York (State)—Utica—Fiction.
I. Title.
PS3562.E4937M87   1999   99-14974
813'.54—dc21   CIP

10 9 8 7 6 5 4 3 2 1

For Jody McAuliffe

and

Maeve—

and for

Gene Nassar,

who invented East Utica

Our souls are like those orphans whose unwedded mothers die in bearing them: the secret of our paternity lies in their grave, and we must there to learn it.

Herman Melville, *Moby-Dick*

To the student of New York history, each family is identified with a set of virtues or a group of achievements.

Famous Families of New York

The Blue Doll

The boy shivers nude in the dark, preparing himself on his eighteenth birthday, this fatal day in the winter of '54, preparing for what, he doesn't know, in longjohns and two pair of socks, woolen shirt and woolen pants, Irish sweater heavier than the pants, ragged black overcoat—heavier than everything. Into one pocket, a red scarf and a half loaf of Italian bread. Into the other, a jar of peanut butter and a hefty jackknife. Laces up an outsized pair of baseball cleats, then to the belt of his long black coat secures with a giant safety pin his game bag—a burlap sack hanging to the ankles, blood-stained and feather-matted within: traces of his offerings to Caterina Spina. Breakfast? He'll eat snow. He'll suck on glittering icicles, hanging from the depressed boughs of pine trees. Pulls on a pair of white cloth gloves as he glances to the far corner of the eight by eight room. Leaning there, the offering of Gregorio Spina: a twelve-gauge shotgun. Pulls down over the ears, down low over the forehead, a hand-knitted white watch cap, the Christmas gift of Melvina Reed. Looks into the long darkened mirror attached to the closet door and a huge frightening figure, the man he wants to be, looks obscurely back. The boy in the dark feels the onset of a distant pleasure. He'll take the shotgun. On his way out when he remembers. Clomps back in and without removing the useless gloves, brushes his teeth with the fury of one who would draw blood.

⟞•◦•⟝

This boy is a Utica boy, who believes his name to be a fake, a boy known as Robert Tagliaferro. So slight of build is he that when properly attired for a deep winter's hunt, the weight of clothes and shotgun together become nearly too much to bear.

Already, at eighteen, he's a legendary woodsman, a deadeye who in the off-season had become a mushroomer so good that Gregorio Spina, east Utica's acknowledged King of Mushrooms, regularly invites him to explore his royal secret places in the hills around the city. "A future murderer," Spina had remarked of him happily to his wife. "I will lie to this orphan and tell him that he is my true son, and that he should live with us. Then when we are too old, he will save us from these cretins who were born with us in Italy, and who now destroy this beautiful city. Let the cretins go back to Shitland!" And his wife had replied, "Yes, let them go back. They disgust me too. But he is not dark enough. To be your son he would need to be more dark." Then Gregorio said, "I believe that he will surprise everybody. Except me. But who cares? By then I will be fucked in the cemetery! More dark? He could not be more dark."

The couple that the boy lives with in an awful tenement, in an ethnically confused section of Utica, are named Melvina and Morris Reed. He calls these good people Aunt and Uncle, who had carried him, they said, in his infancy to Utica. When asked, for the first time, where he was carried *from*, the Reeds had replied, insanely, that they didn't know. The second time (there would be no third), they said, "From someplace else. Why does it matter? You were carried. You're here." They said, "This is the place. This is your place."

In the exhilarating dawn of the hopeless hunt, the Reeds sleep. The Reeds, who are black. The boy, who is ambiguous, and feels his ambiguity, but cannot plumb it, and so regards himself as an inexplicable freak. "In my aspect and in my eyes," he'll learn to say, "you behold all that's best of dark and bright." "Beware," he'll learn to say with a sly small smile, "Tagliaferro comes down like the wolf on the fold." But at eighteen he has not yet learned sufficient craft to frighten with phrases, and with stories to deliver punishment.

The place said to be the boy's is located on the edge of the Italian east side of town, in an area squeezed brutally between Bleecker and Broad, south and north, and running but six short blocks, east and west. In his *Historical Notebook of Utica, New York and New York State in General,* volume one, Robert would name it, many years later, the wedge. Bleecker: Italian-American Main

Street of immigrant merchant princes, led by the nine brothers Cesso, whose ancient family motto was: "We come; we squat; we conquer," and who cheat their friends and even their own aunts and uncles and cousins more easily and frequently than strangers, because true friends and family, stated Primo Cesso, Cesso the First, as historians of Utica refer to him, are too loving to suspect us, and if they do, they are too kind to tell the police. And Broad, with its condemned warehouses, its empty lots of high weeds and abandoned sofas, love seats for sentimental rapists—a street of drifting trash where the people of the wedge are not tempted to walk after dark and which causes the boy to discover the comforts of his place, because there is no other, home to mostly welfare whites named Bagg, Stiggins, Sherman, and Wragg.

Only the boy among them much ventures to the south side of Bleecker, to Mary Street and Spina's domain. Because he has more than the proper sort of surname. He has the looks of a beautiful bronze-toned Neapolitan waif—the sweetness, the curls— and the desire, for as long as he can recall, to live on Mary Street, a move he's suggested many times to Melvina and Morris. To which the Uncle always responds, "Somebody someday is going to mess up your pretty face." And to which the Aunt always responds, "In our colored skin? Honey, not even you could fool those people up there. So what that you're lighter than that Spina's Sicilian son-in-law, who he calls The African? Does that so-called African like to be called The African? They know who you are. Those people specialize in knowing who everybody is who is not their own selves. Because they intend to keep it intact. Follow me? Know the word hymen, hon? That's what they believe in." Robert only says, "You'll see. I'm going to buy Gregorio's house." Melvina says, "When, hon?" Robert says, "Ask Uncle Morris." Uncle Morris says, "When he's pretty no more."

Still dark: bone dry and windless. The temperature in the Mohawk Valley refuses to rise above zero. Shotgun shouldered, the boy descends into streets barely trod for a week and begins the long southerly ascent from Utica's topographical low point, the paved-over swampland of the city's original site, up Bacon, crossing Bleecker, always rising as he crosses Mary, Blandina, Lansing, arrogant Rutger, always higher through levels of increasingly valuable real estate. At last Eagle, then left and due east to the vast rolling public park on Utica's border, crossing stooped over the park's snow fields frozen deep—a speck of black in a sea of white, this is how he prefers to see himself, in the pleasure of his solitude: as if from above, free, staring down upon himself, watching from his still point a black speck moving across desolate sheets of ice. He hugs this image of himself tight, sinks into it, thinking of nothing as he trudges almost contentedly, always east, to the area where Starch Factory Creek skirts the park's far edge, where he'll follow the creek's course up steep Albany Hill, this is the plan, on this of all days, this the object of the hunt: to reach the creek's source, hewing to the snaking course, now inside, now outside city limits, and Robert working hard against his desire to imagine the origin even as he seeks the origin, as if forethought itself were a contaminant.

His cleats dig in good. He climbs through a brushy and wooded terrain, skirting treacherous small chasms in the paradise he had discovered the summer before, in late August. He liked that word very much: *discover.* He felt, when he discovered it, the same way he'd felt that one time when he stood on the small second floor back porch of Gregorio's house, and there were no sounds of voices, or automobiles, or dogs, or even birds, and he could almost touch the massive fruit of the cherry tree arching over toward him, and he could stare down endlessly into the rich little garden, dense with tomatoes, lettuce, and basil, and the rusted tin roof of the shed directly below, between the garden and the house. What was he discovering then? When he told Morris, Morris said, "The shed? Is that what they call the slave quarters?" He didn't tell Morris, because he didn't have the words then, that on Gregorio's back porch, in the silence, he was the only one alive in the whole world, and how good that felt, and how he never felt better, because he was himself the cherry tree, the garden, and the shed, the only one alive.

This lonely place on Albany Hill is too rugged for real estate developers; too ambiguously related to Utica proper for hunters to take a chance; unthinkable for self-respecting trout fishermen; impossible even for Italian picnickers, for whom all pastoral places are potential sites; and ignored, thank God, by those ball-breaking teenagers who come to the park for the purpose of irritating old lady dandelion pickers with drag racing and ceaseless baseball playing, and with shouted obscenities embarrassing all the young lovers parked under the stately elms.

What were the words he had learned in his American history class at Thomas R. Proctor High? Virgin land. He's traversing "virgin land." The history teacher said that "virgin land" was what our country was before "our forefathers came." He wanted to ask his teacher (who was an Italian-American), "Whose forefathers? And who were the foremothers they came into?" Mischievously, in his bad Italian, he told Gregorio about our forefathers who came into virgin land. In dialect, Gregorio shot back, "Must I tell you what a virgin is for?" When he asked Gregorio if they, our first fuckers, had done the job to him, Gregorio, *in culo,* Gregorio nodded, and said: "Why do you think we came to this country, if not for that? In the old country we had no chance. Here, in America, we must spread ourselves wide open, but here we too have the opportunity to become fuckers. America is very beautiful."

These cleats, his greatest idea. Morris's cleats. The shoes of not-his-father. They called the park Proctor. In Utica, they called many things Proctor. Who were Bleecker, Mary, Blandina, Lansing, and Rutger? Where he was now had no name. Working on up the slope, he saw nothing, and was glad. In this terrific cold, only a single, relentless crow. Who gets to say what the names of places will be? That would be something: to become a namer of places. The previous August he'd been thrilled by the density of wild life that he'd encountered in such a small area, never hunted, not even by stray dogs. If he saw a stray dog today in his secret place, for sure he'd shoot it. Now, when he wanted none of the things of August, a jumping brown burst beneath his feet! a streak of brown streaking! and he blasts barrel one and no change of speed and he blasts barrel two: the rabbit tumbles. He approaches to verify what he suspects. That he's shot badly and must now do what he did when he began to hunt at twelve, and shot badly all the time. Hoists the quivering thing by the back legs. Delivers a swift sharp chop to the back of the neck, to grant the mercy of a broken neck, not to sever the head, which is not possible to do, but it happens: a slash of red across the white-gloved left palm, the head sliding slowly down ice, down into the creek. For her *cacciatore* sauce, Caterina will not require the head. To insure freshness, he slits it open all the way to and through the bung hole, removes gloves, rips out guts and tosses them into the creek, so that the guts might join the lonely head, he'll tell Gregorio, who will feel grief for the rabbit even as he forks it down with gusto. Bunny into burlap sack, safe, where it'll freeze rock-hard within an hour. Wipes his hands on the long black coat and resumes his trek, feeling a little depressed, maybe everything was ruined now, not because of what he'd done but because he'd been interrupted. Worse, because he'd let himself become involved in the interruption. Has difficulty feeling his fingers. Wraps the scarf about his face. Hides Gregorio's shotgun under a large bush. Jams his hands into his coat pockets and starts the ascent again, leaning relaxed and deep into the hill, rabbit carcass flopping against the ice. The scarf-mask is not enough. Sharp increase in the angle of ascent; radical narrowing and straightening of the creek's channel. He's leaning deeper, staring into snow. Clearing, looks up and sees it in the clearing. A tiny waterfall, fed by a spring that has groped its way out of the underground, twenty yards above, at the steepest point, just before Albany Hill begins to round itself gently through the breast of its summit. Even in cleats, ice and incline would defeat him at the finish. It's hands and knees now, and when he gets there, finds beside the falls, perfectly encased in a coat of clear ice formed from the water-splash, a doll in a blue dress, shoeless, on her back. The feet are blue. The ankles too. The hands are blue. Cheeks and nose: cracked and red. Eyes open. This. Almost bald. This. Robert Tagliaferro removes the scarf, the water-splash coating his left sleeve and cheek, freezing upon him almost instantly. Removes gloves. With all his might, two-fisted he's punching the air, punching the hill bloody. Picks it up, hugging it to his chest, wrapping it in the scarf, easing it, the blue baby, so stiff, down into the game bag alongside the rabbit carcass. *This is her body.* Who belongs to her? Pieces of downy hair and dress sticking to the ice. He wants to rescue the hair. What else could he do, in this place, on this morning? What was he supposed to do? Leave her there? Leave the hair? With exposed fingers, picks at hair in the ice, picks at dress fragments in the ice, sitting beside the falls, smearing the ice red. Game bag on his lap, dress fragments safely secured within, pushes off sliding and down he goes, screaming, quickly gaining speed out of control over bumps and clumps of brush, screaming and crashing at last to a rest, still screaming, against the large bush of the shotgun. Looks inside the game bag. The ice-coating has shattered; her face is turned into the rabbit's cavity. He rearranges. Covers her as best he can with the red scarf. Transfers peanut butter and bread to sack. Then for a long time stares down into the sack, his entire head almost out of sight. Melvina's white watch cap peeping out.

11:30 A.M. Reaches again the corner of Bacon and Mary. Two doors away, the Spina house, 1303 Mary Street. Gregorio, sitting at the kitchen table, has spied him walking through the alley. Robert knocks. Caterina, alerted by her husband to the visitor's identity, steps into character: "Who's there?" Gregorio, with excessive volume, says, "Our black son!" Robert responds in heavily accented English: "Santee Clothes." Then the door, dead-bolted day and night in this crime-free neighborhood, swings open wide and he enters as she grins and tells him that she's been a good Christian and deserves a present on this morning of God's wrath. He hesitates. He reaches in. Pulls out the carcass of the rabbit. She says, in mock sadness, "Only one?" Shall he do it? He reaches in. Gives her the frozen bread. Gregorio says, "In all things, my wife is impossible to satisfy." The wife replies, "I should make my husband eat this bread like a stone. I'm going to divorce him," as she pours Robert a cup of espresso and refills her husband's cup, who says: "Your coffee is no good," then takes it down in one swallow and says, "Ah!" Robert says, "Yes, divorce him tomorrow in honor of your fiftieth wedding anniversary." *La commedia è finita.*

She lays before Robert an array of his favorite things: a hunk of salami, a loaf of freshly baked bread, a dish of roasted sweet peppers sunk in olive oil, a jug of Gregorio's homemade wine, and two cannoli. He says, "Please forgive me. I cannot." Dips a finger into the olive oil. Sucks it. Says again, "I cannot." She says, with real pain, "You don't like what I put on the table?" Gregorio says, "To the Devil with him, he is fasting for communion." She replies, "But he's not a Catholic," as she watches Gregorio dig into the peppers. "Pig!" she says, "you ate twenty minutes ago!" Gregorio says, "I am fulfilling my pig nature. He has no appetite. How can this boy, who eats like he doesn't like to eat, be my son?" "Thank you," Robert says, in English, "now we can begin our friendship." Caterina, who has no English, asks, "What did he say?" Her husband responds, in Italian: "He says that for our health it is much better never to have been a member of a family." Caterina says, "Look at his knuckles. They bleed."

Robert spends the afternoon curled about his burlap sack, on a pew at St. Anthony's, one block from home.

Late that night, carrying Morris's claw hammer, he returns to 1303 Mary Street. And then this boy, who had long cradled himself in the fangs of an incurable idea—that he, himself, was a thrown-away child—hacks up with difficulty the frozen turf of the shed floor and buries the thrown-away child, his scarf, and the jar of peanut butter.

When he returns home, very late, Melvina and Morris greet him at the door in their pajamas. They couldn't imagine where he was at such an hour. "Robert, we were so afraid something happened." *[Pause.]* "I made you a birthday pie." Robert, looking full at the terrorized Reeds, says, "I'm sick of being treated like a baby. I'm eighteen." Melvina says, "I'll make you a chicken sandwich, hon, and there's still some chocolate cream pie." Robert, who hasn't eaten all day, says, "I'm not hungry." The three of them, standing in the doorway, stare at the floor. Then Morris says, "Let's leave him alone. Let's go to bed."

There had been no news reports of missing children, distraught mothers and fathers, kidnappings, ransom notes. Nobody knew, except for Robert Tagliaferro, and the parent who did it.

Chapter 1

Robert Tagliaferro, at sixty, sits in his room under a single bulb of small wattage, setting ten mouse traps. Tonight, for the first time, without bait. A cot, a miniature refrigerator, a clothes tree, a hot plate. On the wall behind him, an engineer's map of Utica, three feet by two feet. On the wall before him, many photos of himself, arranged chronologically in neat rows, one for each year since 1954, when shortly after graduation from Proctor High, in the interminable night of Utica's terminal illness, he disappeared.

Glances up at wall of photos. Smiles slyly. Speaks: "I know thee not."

The room is located in lower Manhattan, on the basement floor of one of New York's oldest used book stores, where Robert has worked since day two in the city. On day three, he told the store's manager, "I have to work around the clock." From nine to six, he'd continue to shelve and watch for thieves. After hours, he promised to sweep, dust, straighten all the books to the perpendicular, wash windows and floors, feed the two cats, control the mouse population. At two and four A.M., without fail, he'd check the traps. Re-arm as necessary. Dispose of bodies. Above all, to protect and perfect the alphabetical order of things, this would be his devotion. He actually said the words "to the perpendicular." He, an eighteen year old only recently out of Utica, actually said "the alphabetical order of things" and "my devotion." The manager was intimidated; he was fascinated; he was losing his will.

Just off the impressive basement section on New York State History, Robert had noticed, on day two, a small windowless room, empty except for three filing cabinets of old accounting records and a sink with a single faucet, running cold. He noticed and he saw his future. No increase in pay would be necessary, no benefits would be requested, if he could but live rent and utility free in that room. He'd use (and twice daily clean) the customer's rest room. Take nightly spartan sponge baths at his cold water sink as a consideration to the public. A man on guard twenty-four hours a day, seven days a week. A man waiting in his waiting room, preparing the life to come by feeding steadily upon his own innards, and calling it, "My voyage in American history."

The manager said that he would consult the owner. In fact, the manager was the owner and wanted a month to observe this beautiful young man, who was probably crazy. When the month was up, the manager concluded that Robert was certainly crazy— the most he'd say was yes or no or okay by me. Never thank you. Never good morning or good night or excuse me. This boy who seemed to own but three shirts and two pair of washable pants, who wore no socks, a practice continued even through the cold months. The manager felt that he did not have the right to raise the question of intimate apparel. The boy was harmless. Three men for the price of one, regardless of the condition of the lower undergarments, if they existed, which he doubted, so who cares why the boy wanted to live in the store?

In the first year, Robert would accidentally spring a trap in his hands on the average of twice a week. Almost reluctantly, he developed a technique that reduced these painful incidents to two per month. Nevertheless: forty-two years of accidental springings. Smash. One thousand times. Smash. The fingers rebelled; developed a life of their own; thickened and roughened themselves grotesquely with fibroid tissue. Robert speaks: "Give us a touch, Robert." He laughs. Who'd want to be touched, or probed, by those things, all finger nails long gone? "Not I," says Robert.

Tonight, no flinches, no grimaces as he coolly springs a trap for each finger. Lifts the trap-laden hands before his eyes. He's not unhappy. Lowers hands. He's sitting there at his dining table desk, relaxed, just gazing at his ten trapped fingers, pleased to remind himself that he no longer feels pain. Gregorio and Caterina were long dead, or well over a hundred and living in Florida. He was betting dead. The Utica city directory, which he'd consulted regularly since 1980, had listed only a Morris Reed after 1986. Divorced? Impossible. Melvina was dead. *What color is it now, her colored skin?* Again, lifts his hands before his eyes. Hold. Gazing. Hold. Hold. Lowers hands to table. Frees each of his fingers, the first one with his teeth. Dons reading glasses. Arises and approaches the wall of photos to begin his ritual survey. At base of wall, picks up a long black-barreled flashlight and says, as he rises, "All the better to see you with, my dear." Smiles a little as he lays a fat forefinger on the most recent of the photos. Speaks: "His Ugliness, Robert Tagliaferro, I salute thee." He likes so much having said it that he says it again.

In his room, at night, often and at length, Robert talks to himself, but not out of madness. He talks to himself because he fears for his vocal chords. That they might wither, become dangerously brittle over the years of disuse, and for what he must do he requires not merely a voice but an unusual voice, one capable of a range of effects. For the last two years, his training—the final phase, as he thinks of it—has consisted in reading aloud, six nights a week, three hours per night, from Shakespeare's late tragedies and Washington Irving's *History of New York*. For forty-two years he has prepared for the happy time to come by reserving Sunday evenings exclusively for systematic and dramatic renderings of *Webster's Unabridged*.

Taped to dining table desk:

> Breakfast (in room)
> small bowl cold bran cereal (for regularity)
> collection of lyric poetry (any period)
> one cup coffee (black)
>
> Lunch (in room)
> classic novel (pre-1900)
> four saltine crackers
> one glass water
> two bananas (for reduction of B.M. frequency)
> one Hostess cupcake (cream-filled, chocolate)
> reserve second cup cake
>
> Dinner
> undistinguished chop or steak
> mashed potatoes (gravyless)
> green vegetable (undressed)
> tomato salad (undressed)
> roll (dry)
> one glass water

Dinner is braved without literary support, in a nearby cheap restaurant, eyes on counter fixed, shoveling it in like a starving man—his voraciousness motivated not by hunger but by desire to return to his room, where he relishes the nights, when notes are taken so much more pleasurably than food. In monomania, he's all athirst for the fatherly, the first things. In his room, he's preparing for re-entry.

Bedtime Snack: 11:45 P.M. (sharp)
second Hostess cup cake

In view of the facts of his life, to say that Robert Tagliaferro
has no friends "in New York" paints a picture almost of normal-
ity: That this man of absence has toured about in the great city,
experiencing the shocking presence of its various scenes. The
truth is that in forty-two years he has but rarely left the environs
of the bookstore. Neither man nor woman has he known since
escaping from Utica a virgin—he, a virgin yet at sixty, who
embraces images as he drifts toward sleep. So many nameless faces
from the street and store, all beautiful, so many toward him drift
in sleep's requital. Upon waking, he's consoled by the haunted
words of Yeats, which he quotes often, and aloud, doubling his
consolation with the sounds of words:

> boys and girls, pale from the imagined love
> Of solitary beds . . .

He's staring at his latest photo. Speaks: "And is it you, Rip?"
One by one begins to take them all in, starting with the eighteen-
year-old, lingering on each image while working hard to gather
into focus the image just preceding and the image about to come,
time past and time future. *I persist.* The eighteen-year-old father
to the man of sixty. Again, the eighteen-year-old. A long, long
look. Closes eyes. Feels way to number forty-two. Eyes open.
Lovely. Speaks: "For Robert? What is Robert to me, or me to
Robert, that I should weep for him?" This totally bald man, of
bleached-out complexion, almost as white as a cue ball. Bony
face. Protruded, thick-lipped sensuality. Dark heavy bags under
the eyes. He's smiling: "Alas, poor Robert, I knew him." Glances
over to photo number one, the boy that girls of his youth should
have squealed for. Back onto photo number forty-two: "*Io te
saluto.* In Utica, we are unknown."

At dawn, he'll carry to the street three large suitcases and one
small one. The small one for clothes and toiletries. The three large

ones for the ninety thick notebooks containing in a minute script illegible to all but himself the fruits of forty-two years of research in the history of Utica and New York state, from the coming of the Dutch to the present. At dawn, a cab will carry him to Port Authority and the bus that will carry him on, north to Utica, forty-two years to the day since he left. And he'll leave Manhattan almost as he'd left Utica. Without giving notice, forwarding address unknown. The difference would be this: he'd left Utica with twelve dollars in his pocket. At dawn, he leaves Manhattan with last week's salary in cash (two hundred dollars), and the savings of his monkish life, a certified check of fabulous magnitude.

Chapter 2

"Utica Utica Utica! What a town!" and he's jerked forward hard against the seatbelt, up from sleep by the big-voiced driver's heavy-footed finish at the Greyhound depot on Main. "What a beautiful town!" A soft rain, the place itself, and Robert Tagliaferro in the warm dark delivered to consciousness and home, evicted, remembering a snatch of conversation overheard in the Port Authority waiting area: "Albany? The asshole of New York state, and Troy is nine miles up." "How far up is Utica?" "Ithaca?" "I tend to pronounce it 'Utica.'" All day long on the New York State Thruway, how haunted he was by the forgotten familiars of his hunting days in the Mohawk Valley, how dreadful it had been to see them again: naked children chasing ducks and geese into a muddy farm pond; fly-agitated, dungy cows; wild flowers and paranoid woodchucks; green fields and abandoned barns. Razors on a lidless eye.

Robert and a young man in his middle twenties, a six-footer carrying one bag, tanned, muscular, and gloom shrouded, alone disembark at Utica. The young man offers to help Robert with his four to the taxi lane. Robert leans over and examines the tag on the young man's bag. Still leaning, he responds: "The tag on your bag tells a lie." No reply. Robert, rising, extends his hand: "Call me Bobby Forza. We owe our meeting to the gods. Look past my manner and appearance, Mr. Alexander Lucas, so-called." With a touch of theatrical menace, the young man tears the identification tag from his bag, crumples it, then stuffs it roughly into the breast pocket of Robert's mangy blazer. Robert, undeterred: "You stand before the world in disguise, sir, as do I. But does the world take notice? I have deprived myself of human intercourse, carnal and otherwise. I have been too much in my being pent. You, who refuse to shake my hand, on the other hand—"

"Forget it."

"You, sir, who were, for a time, in New York City—"

"Forget it."

"Sexual intrigue, sir?"

"Mr. Forza."

"Sexual intrigue?"

"I'm going." *[He does not move.]*

"Does Mrs. Lucas know?"

"Mrs. Lucas is dead."

"Oh, Mr. Lucas."

"Oh yeah."

[Pause.]

"Mr. Lucas, alas."

"Happy now?"

[Pause.]

"Forgive me."

"How do you spell that?"

They stare past one another. The man who calls himself Forza extends his hand again. The man who calls himself Lucas accepts it, saying: "Madness is taking place." The older man says, "Forgive me for smiling. In your grief you retain your wit. You tend to pronounce it 'Utica.' Forgive me, sir, for laughing. You don't wear your heart on your short sleeve shirt, and here I stand in my stupid cruelty, beneath this overhanging thing, which I don't know the word for, and there you stand, sir, in the rain. Like you, Mr. Lucas, I am not happy. Come in under this thing, Mr. Lucas. A brave young person with a sense of humor in the midst of personal disaster—"

"I'm okay where I am."

"I note that you continue to wear a wedding band. You are not okay where you are."

"I'm going."

"You are not going, Mr. Lucas. You haven't moved. You're staying. Have you not begun to unburden yourself to a foolish stranger, of that which young persons should not be forced to bear? Your beautiful wife is dead. Of her beauty I am certain. She died. Permit me a glimpse of her picture in your wallet."

"You nuts?"

"Permit me."

"I can't."

"Wherein lies the harm?"

"I never had one made."

"It's not too late. Have one made tomorrow. Have several made. Then place them strategically about your dwelling and they will sustain you in your desire to dwell morbidly. Mr. Lucas, you too are nuts. In my time, I had forty-two wallet pictures made. The cause of death, Mr. Lucas?"

"Fucking."

"How now?"

"Fucking."

"Mr. Lucas?"

"You deaf?"

"Mr. Lucas, I heard the word. I know the word. Recall that you converse with a person of perfect inexperience."

[Pause.]

"Goddamn you."

"Yes. It would only be just."

[Pause.]

"Goddamn me too."

"We'll amuse each other in hell."

"No. *[Pause.]* I'll amuse you now. Try to visualize Caroline Lucas, three minutes old and filthy with fluids of several colors, sucking hard on my wife's breast, who's still in the stirrups, wide open and grinning, we're all grinning in that room, joking about the baby's innate sucking knowledge, when it pours out of her vagina like a blood-faucet suddenly turned on full blast. Are we amused? When the current Caroline is twenty minutes old, they stop working on the former Caroline Lucas, but the baby's still sucking hard, because who had the time in that situation to pull her off? Are you visualizing? My wife got what she wanted. She had a baby. Then she bled to death in her happiness. Mr. Forza, I believe that you bled to death too. It would account for the corpse-like quality of your complexion. On her first birthday, I brought her to my wife's sister, in New York. A year ago yesterday. For good. Feel better now? Can you say 'fucking,' old man?"

"Mr. Lucas, I am capable of saying anything. Come in under this overhanging thing, whatever it is called."

"That overhanging thing is called the overhang."

"Your hair is soaked. Your face glistens under the street lamp with streaks of rain. I do not feel better, to answer your question. I will not say that word, to answer your other question, and now look at you! You exude the glamour of an intense movie actor, in a sad and humid location. Mr. Lucas, fear me not. I am just an old virgin, a skinny runt aflame in his asexuality. We have told secrets of ourselves. I will tell you many, many more, of our origins, and of this formerly fair city. Your shirt, Mr. Lucas. It drips with rain."

"Here comes your cab, Mr. Forza."

"What was it you would teach about sexual love? Somehow it escaped me."

"Your cab, Mr. Forza."

"How harsh your formality is to me. We are not cold, are we Alessandro? We do not belong to the frigid ethnicities. How long I've wanted someone to call me Bobby!"

"Forget it."

"Wherein lies the harm?"

"No."

"Dismiss the cab, Alessandro. I have no place to go, unless you would be so kind, during this, my transition phase—"

"Fuck it."

"Certainly! But your blood has its own design upon you. The virtues of the fathers will be visited even upon the sons who say 'fuck it.' Ah, look! Alessandro Lucca the fifth, he comes from the rain, our reluctant player, secretly named for the heroic progenitor."

"Why should you have to go to a hotel?"

"You tell me, Alessandro."

"Why shouldn't I take in a total stranger, who is totally insane? Am I a heartless bastard? Wait here, don't leave. Because I'm about to do the logical thing."

"I won't leave."

"I'll be right back with the car, because I don't give a shit."

"I'll be here. Unmoving. Under this thing, the overhang."

"The Ancient Mariner and me, the asshole wedding guest."

Lucas goes. When he's out of sight, Robert makes a 360 degree surveillance of the area. No one. Good. Maybe he'll give it a try. The trip had been endless. Scheduled stops in Kingston, Albany, and Schenectady, and a four-hour breakdown nine miles north of Albany, in Troy. He'd been so frustrated by the delay that, with people all about, he almost did it in the bus station in Troy. Glances at watch. Nine-thirty P.M. Historic Bagg's Square. Central shabbiness. Nothing. There should be some car traffic, a staggering drunk, a couple strolling in the soft rain without umbrella, kissing long under a street lamp. Hears the sound of a distant siren. Utica noir. Do it at last, projecting deep into the theater. Another 360-degree check. Stifles a giggle. Then sends his burnished baritone, surprisingly hefty, floating out into the middle distance and beyond, bearing the lightest touch of bombast:

> A terse, and a salty tongue, most unlike my own.
> Mark him well, this widower,
> Self-anointed the heartless one.
> How it delights him
> To affect the barbarian!
> This reader of Coleridge,
> This real estate agent,
> In a dying town. *[Pause.]*
> Who speaks for heartless bastards?
> Not I, said the bastard. *[Pause.]*
> Before this night is out, he'll call me Bobby.

In a honey gold, '78 Dodge four door, with a defunct defroster, the driver's side windshield wiper operating on its slowest speed only, and the other bearing evidence of having been broken off violently, they pull away just as the rain turns torrential, Lucas saying, "I can't see all of a sudden," and Forza: "Alessandro, I can navigate this town blindfolded," and then Lucas in a crafted monotone: "Bobby, I'll call you Bobby and you'd better call me Alex, or I'll throw your ass out at the next light, which I can't see!" *[losing monotone]* "Jesus! I better pull over."

"Stay the course, Alexander."

"Where's the son of bitch intersection?"

"Trust your navigator. When I say 'three,' turn right. Only on three."

"Fuck it. I'll kill us both."

"Where do you live, Alexander?"

"Pellettieri Ave."

"Correct. THREE! Well done. Where on Pellettieri Ave? Near Joe's?"

"Across from Joe's. What the hell happened to one and two? You know Joe's?"

"When I say 'three,' turn left. I've dreamt of Joe's for forty-two years. THREE! Well done. I've been gone for forty-two years, Alexander. We've now achieved Bleecker and proceed in a condition of zero visibility, in an easterly direction, deeply east we travel, at perhaps seven miles per hour. THREE!"

"WHAT FUCKING DIRECTION!?"

"I was only fooling, Alexander. [*Pause.*] It is established, is it not? You appear to give something of a shit."

"I'm lost in my goddamn home town."

"Splendid! Our tragic theme, imaginatively phrased. EIGHT!"

"In the hands of a maniac."

"When I say 'now,' count to three and turn left. [*Pause.*] Alexander."

"What?"

"Now."

[*Turn executed.*]

"We're here, Mr. Forza."

"We are."

"And Joe's is still open."

"It is."

"Hungry?"

"I desire succulent goat."

"You can't get that here."

"But they have it, this I know."

"They have it, but *you* can't get that here. [*Pause.*] Hey. I have to clear something up. I lied."

"Later. I'm starving."

"I won't call you Bobby. Never. It'll never happen."

"My friend is a prophet."

They're walking into Joe's and twenty-three seconds later they're walking out in haste, at least Lucas is, who's pulling Forza along, glancing over his shoulder, and saying: "You're lucky those people know me."

Chapter 3

This curious man, all made of words, who hasn't yet revealed himself to the Samaritan of reluctant goodness, is rifling through correspondence, he's peeking into desk drawers and filing cabinets in the office of Lucas Realty and Rentals, first floor occupant of a narrow two-family house, opposite Joe's, searching for some trace of the intimate life and family history of the young man he's unmasked as Alessandro Lucca, who moves now above him, in the kitchen of his second-floor apartment, preparing a late meal. *No use.* Goes to back room. Lies on couch that will serve as his bed. Looks up suddenly in terror at the ceiling. Thunder in the ceiling. The house shakes. The man above sounds as if he's about to stomp himself through. Then Robert remembers. Smiles a little and turns on his side, closes his eyes, pulls up his knees. Baby Tagliaferro, trying to relax. These flimsy structures endure too, like Utica's Rutger Street mansions of eternal stone. The house is shaking because someone is at home.

Robert carries his toiletries halfway down a short hall to the bathroom of the deep, free-standing, and gargoyle-footed tub. Washes the bald dome and face, brushes his teeth with old-time fury, then looks in the mirror, nods and decides not to shave. Decides that a woman is yet possible. That she must be possible. Decides that his long-preserved virginity may at last be tried. Speaks to the mirror: "Let us modify the horror of ourself with a beard." Tomorrow the tub, hot, almost too hot, almost to the brim, then slowly, slowly submerge to the neck, the gargoyle head afloat, as if by the surface of water severed. Imagines another tub scene. Not soon to be realized: water just below the waist, opposite a Rubens-like female, the skinny man gripped in her thighs, cock bobbing tumescent. Speaks to tub: "A consummation devoutly to be wished." Thickening (some) in crotch.

Climbs stairs at back foyer, inhaling essence of garlic. Garlic going gold in olive oil. Before he can knock, the young man opens the door. Blank looks exchanged in greeting. Young man to stove. Robert approaches: "Alex, I am overcome with remembrance of things past. Spaghetti *aglio e olio.*" Staring at the stove, Alex, affectless: "Spare me the wop gesture. And the Proust cliché." Robert picks up the bottle of olive oil: "A condition equivalent to my own. Extra-virgin."

"Mr. Forza."

"Yes?"

"Stop."

"I need to tell you the truth about myself, Alex."

"Try to stop."

"I entrust you with my secret, Alex. My name is Robert Tagliaferro, and in disguise I've returned after forty-two years to the Sin City of the East, scene of numerous unsolved murders."

"Talking like a book."

"About the past, Alex."

"I've heard it before."

"You'll hear it again and again. This is the point of the past. To unfit us for the present. Alex, there is nothing else to talk about."

"Do me a favor, Mr. Forza."

"The past refuses to spare us."

"Mr. Forza."

"You will not be spared, Alex."

"Hey!"

"Yes?"

"Say garlic and oil."

"Forgetting the past is not a matter of changing the words."

Alex, like a tough guy, pointing: "See this? This. You know what this is?"

[Pause.]

"I have irritated you, Alex. Forgive me."

"Answer me."

Robert takes a risk: "I tremble."

Alex, working harder on tough: "Say the words or you go fucking hungry."

"Your delicious sauce of garlic and oil, lucidly spiced with oregano and salt, much freshly ground black pepper, and a dash, no! a splash of scorching pepperoncini. Alex! Are those the words? And Romano cheese too, to be sprinkled lightly all over, and fresh parsley, coarsely chopped! Alex! How many more words?"

With a spaghetti claw, Alex removes a single strand of pasta from the boiling water. Chews.

"How much longer?"

Alex smiles an actually friendly smile and says, with a little bit of mirth, "Let's eat this in the present."

Then it sets in: the bluntness and outrageousness of their meeting. The sudden intimacy. Finally they're caught, and they sit in silence, embarrassed, hiding in the eating: a pound of pasta, a salad of tomatoes and cucumbers, large enough for six, a king-sized loaf of

Rintrona's Italian bread, and a tall water glass each of Gallo's Hearty Burgundy. In order to extend the silence as long as possible, they eat far beyond their appetites. They eat everything. When the assault is completed, Robert leans back, exhausted, glassy-eyed, and says, "Ah, Alex, you're a prince. Alex, I can't move, Christ in heaven." *[Stifles a burp.]* Alex, almost kindly, says, "Mr. Forza, I'll have to be direct. Excuse me. I'll keep your secret, because I don't care who you are. The Lucca background was obliterated almost a hundred years ago. This is what we wanted in our family, and this is what I want for myself. *[Refills glasses to brim.]* How do you know the Lucca background?"

"I have a method. *[Pause.]* After the death of the grandfather of your grandfather, the name of Lucca could be found only on a tombstone in Calvary Cemetery. Do you visit the grave, Alex? To trim away the weeds on a monthly basis?"

"Tell me how you know and you win a month here free, plus I find you a cheap apartment in the elegant Cornhill district."

"In the district of pyromaniacs! Thank you. You would find me an apartment in the burgeoning African-American community."

"Get a little sun, Mr. Forza, get a gun, and you'll pass. It's cheap up there now. Eventually the Vietnamese and the Bosnians drive them out. Order is restored. Eventually the real estate values sky, because eventually they always sky. That's where I'd buy myself, if I had the money. In the Cornhill district. *[Pause.]* Pellettieri Ave has become a hole."

"I have the money, but my heart is set on 1303 Mary Street."

"Not for sale."

"By memory you know all of the For Sale signs of Utica?!"

"The eastern extremity of Mary Street is never for sale. This is known. It's a stronghold in there. One block away, down on Bleecker, they have monthly shotgun murders on the street. We chalk it up to the exuberance of the Hispanic community. They had blood on Bleecker frozen in the ice for a week last winter.

The values plunge. But guess what? The Italians of the eastern
extremity of Mary do not give a shit about the values. Nobody
moves. Those people are trees. On Mary Street, materialism is
scorned. On the thirteen hundred block of Mary, they hose down
the sidewalks nightly and at dawn. They paint the exteriors every
third year. You better not spit on their sidewalks. Between the
sidewalk and the curb, religious art is installed. Do not spit in the
vicinity of the Virgin. The Astroturf is laid in, which no dog dares
to shit upon. They kill and eat the dog. Even the owner of the
dog they kill and eat. If it's their own relation, they cook him in
the most expensive olive oil. The source of their power is the
freedom granted to each by each to express yourself without
restraint if your neighbor's dog shits on your personal Astroturf.
This is well-known amongst those people. They call it a culture.
They call it a community, and it accounts for their courtly man-
ners and the respect they show each other, because their com-
mandment is, Love thy Neighbor as Thyself, or risk a richly
deserved death. On Mary Street, they prove one thing conclusively. Fear is good. Fear creates kindness. Fear creates love itself.
They have proved this on the eastern extremity. You know why
the blacks are drawn to Mary Street? Why they want proximity?
Because they need to study the masters of cold violence. Black
violence is hot and sloppy and the blacks know this. They don't
want the Italians out. They want to live side by side. They're
infatuated, which proves something conclusively about the blacks."

"What does it prove?"

"They're assholes."

"Alex, eventually even the old Italians of Mary Street die.
Gregorio Spina is dead."

"But Sebastian Spina lives. The grandchildren move in the
same day as the funeral. These people think they possess decisive
fire power. They go up to the Deerfield Fish and Game Club and
zero in the rifles and handguns. After mass, every Sunday. My
source tells me they have a military issue weapon capable of 300

rounds per minute. These people believe they're ready, but I believe they're wrong. The subcultures will overrun their position. Like the Chinese, they'll throw their sad and worn-out bodies on the barbed wire, so that their children can swarm in. What are we talking about? What do the fucking Chinese have to do with this? Mr. Forza, let's get back on track. Show some gratitude. I think you owe me an answer. How do you know the Lucca background?"

"Let's say 1303 came up for sale. What would it cost?"

"Thirty-five, tops."

"Tomorrow I give you seventy large in cash. Then you do something for me. Do this. Go to the owner of 1303, the cocksucker. On behalf of Robert Forza, plank down the seventy large in cash. When you plank it down, say, 'Hey! Fuck me!!' Tell him you'll take no commission, which I privately kick in on the side, under the table. Offer Sebastian Spina seventy large. The cunt won't scorn it. The good alderman, Signor Cagato. Mr. He Hath Shat. Now am I talking like a fucking book, Alex?"

"Imitation Scorsese."

"You are in awe of those people on Mary Street, are you not?"

"They disgust me."

"You feel alternating disgust and admiration, do you not?"

"I hate those people. I hope the subcultures destroy them in my lifetime. Are you going to answer my question?"

"Alex, you will witness a destruction. I promise. And now I will answer your question. The Uticans do not read books. Please, Alex. [*Pause.*] Please. Have patience with my method. Do not leave the room. They do not read books. This is their strength. It is an astonishment, but true, that nine histories of Utica have been written. No city of comparable size in this country has nine histories of its own. Massive cities, Detroit and Miami, have only four each. Nine! This fact alone tells us that Utica is quite rare. Like a vicious and mysterious disease. Each history written by a different subcultural scribe, searching for a cure, by his own people unread, by his own people ridiculed as a fairy. But read by me. And this is my method. I read. Nine subcultures; nine stories of a city. Alessandro the First is in the books. That is how I know. More or less. City directories published annually since 1817. Archival materials concerning land acquisitions by Utica's founding fathers. The tons of dusty and mildewed records of swindlings and charitable donations. First the swindlings. Then the charity. Then streets named in their honor. These things make your nose run. You sneeze and cough and wheeze, because the historical record is an upper respiratory disease. By the carton they are stored in the New York Public Library. The manuscripts, the books, the documents, the loose pages, the privately printed monographs, the diaries of women incarcerated in the Utica Lunatic Asylum, taking their meals in what they called a water closet. In the nineteenth century, they were allowed to call them lunatics, who they made eat in a toilet. And I have read it all. The stench of this stuff! The map of this city of slow death is a clear and present image in the middle of my mind. You say that Pellettieri Ave has become a hole. But I shall teach you that it was part of the original hole, the site of Utica before the white man came. In becoming a hole, Pellettieri Ave is only becoming itself again. Be of good cheer, Alex. We may yet rejoice. *[Pause.]* The Uticans do not read. *[Pause. Belches. Unbuckles belt. Belches.]* They complain. They whine and they moan about the degradation of the city. The subcultures, in the meanwhile, feed upon each other and themselves. *[Pause. Epic belch. Undoes top button of pants.]* The subcultures will stop their murders and fires. They always do. They will also stop the dope, believe it or not. They will become American property owners and complainers, and they will zero in the rifles in Deerfield, but they will not shoot again. Nevermore! And this is their tragedy. No more shooting and stabbing! We are cannibals first. Then we advance. We become whiners, and eat self-pity. I read. You have read, but not in the historical fields.

You have read in the literary fields, and this is your joy and grief and limitation. Yes, to use your spicy language, you are the asshole wedding guest, and I am the Ancient Mariner who will teach you, and a few others, who are yet to be revealed. The grandfather of your grandfather was destroyed by Italian blood. In some vague and worthless way you know this. I read it in a book. In a manner of speaking. His children buried his name because they decided that it would be a far, far better thing to be eaten by strangers. *[Pauses. Stands. Says, "Oh, my stomach." Sits. Alex says, "Mr. Forza, may I assist you in any way?" Robert says, "You may not."]* A subculture, Alex, is a self-consuming cancer. Alessandro number one learned that the most hideous of humans were his own countrymen, not because the Italians are the devils of this earth, but because they were his own people. Oh how they suffered with him at his wife's death! They shed actual tears, and then they pulled out his intestines, and they ate them, a foot at a time, and how enraged they became when he refused to give them his handkerchief so that they could wipe their bloody mouths. To survive inside the ethnic group you must become like excrement itself, toward which alone the group feels no jealousy. Smear thyself with shit, and live! Because it is recorded in the histories that not even the subcultures will eat shit. The Italians, like the Dutch and the English and the Germans and the Irish before them, drew the line there. No shit eating. This we will not do. And it is thus that a germ of humanity is born in the subcultures. Alessandro number one refused to make himself excremental. And so your ancestors buried him in the Protestant cemetery among the founders of this city. They hid him in Calvary, where no Italian walks. *[Pauses. Suddenly doubles over. Face to knees. Stands. Continues, pacing.]* The rendings, Alex, the gnashing of the teeth, the smacking of the lips. *[Pauses. To sink. Bends over sink. Mouth open, as if to vomit. Dry heaves. Straightens. Awash in sweat.]* Have you watched these people eat? By law, they should be forced to eat in public, in athletic arenas, so that the others, the moaners, may learn. Eat thy neighbor raw. *[Gags.]* This you almost understand, Alex. Your people did not wish to pass. They wished to escape the true power of history. Subcultural power. They failed, of course. They became decent. They were ignored. Like the Anglo-Saxons, the Italians on Mary Street will not shoot. They zero in the rifles on Sundays so that they don't have to shoot themselves. They have seen their grandchildren to college and they have begun to lose their appetite. Spina will accept my money, but you must not tell him that you represent a well-spoken gentleman named Forza. You must tell him that you represent a nigger. Just as he is about to sign the papers for the seventy thousand, you must tell him that this is the nigger money of a thick-lips. Then show him the cash. Turn the bag of money upside down and let it fall all over the floor just before he signs, and say, 'You will sign now for the nigger money and become the first wop inside the stronghold to yield to the nigger element.' Now I am finished! Alex! I need assistance!!"

Robert, red-faced and sweat-soaked, may lose control. He's afraid to take long steps. He feels the imminence of explosive expulsion, perhaps from both ends. Alex says, "First door on your left." Robert moves stiff-legged down the hall. Alex decides that, in the meanwhile, he'll clear the dishes from the table. He decides to wash the dishes. No Robert. Hey! Might as well dry them too. No Robert. Puts dishes away. Cleans stove. This old man is in trouble. Puts on a pot of coffee. Fills four cannoli shells. Still no Robert. Did he die in there? Then he re-appears, looking more corpse-like than ever, and walking like a patient on his feet for the first time since undergoing major abdominal surgery. Alex says, "You doing okay?" Robert says, "I think that I need something." Robert pauses, then adds: "But I don't know the name of the thing that I need." Alex says, "It's not Alka-Seltzer." Robert says, "I know Alka-Seltzer. It's not Alka-Seltzer." Alex says, "You need to drink water." Robert says, "I know the name of water. That's not what I need." Alex says, "In my opinion, water is the name of the thing you need." Robert says, "I think it's Pepsi Cola." Alex says, "You don't want Pepsi Cola. Either it's the water, or something that sounds like Pepsi Cola, but which is a very different thing. The fact that you know the name of water doesn't mean that you don't need water. You better drink a big glass, or take that other thing, which I have in the cabinet in the bathroom. Which is where I'm not about to go into at this time, or even an hour from now. If you want it bad enough, you have to go in there all by yourself and get the Pepto-Bismol. Don't expect me, as the host, to do this for you, the guest." Robert says, "Pepto-Bismol. Yes. That's the name of the thing I need." Robert says, "I myself fear to go back in." Alex says, "In the cabinet over the sink in there, you'll find a can of Irish Springtime. Be prodigal."

When Robert returns, he finds that Alex has poured the espresso and placed between them the four cannoli. Robert is afraid to sit. Or stand. Robert only says, very softly, "Alex." Alex says, "But I can. Watch." Robert watches in amazement, fighting the nausea. Robert, as Alex eats: "You did not buy these cannoli from the wonderful Carmen Caruso. Somebody made them at home. Somebody filled them only a few minutes ago. Now somebody is about to wolf his third cannoli. I have never seen a man eat three cannoli in one sitting. Perhaps this man will save me number four for breakfast." Alex says, "It's possible."

Almost midnight. Robert says, "You do your real estate business under the noses of the cretinous inheritors of those who destroyed him. The secret Italian real estate agent. But who, aside from me, cares? I must retire now. I must go. *[Pause.]* He, the tragic progenitor. The grandfather of your grandfather, so gentle and so generous. Goodnight, Alex. He was a bull. I must go now. Goodnight, my charitable friend. A tremendous bull. The neck on the man! It was said that in girth it measured twenty inches. Alex, look at my neck. Can you guess the girth?" Alex says, "Mr. Forza, relax. You don't have a chicken neck. I guess thirteen." Robert touches his throat and says, "Thirteen is correct, plus this loose hanging skin. Goodnight." Alex says, "See you in the morning." Robert, at the door, wants to say much more, but he says nothing.

Blank looks exchanged in farewell.

[Sounds of several distant sirens.]

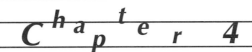

Chapter 4

Just before noon of the following day, after a startling morning up on Mary Street, and higher elevations (Rutger, upper Mohawk, the Parkway), Alex Lucas returns to the hole of Pellettieri Ave and bangs shut the front door of his realty office, shouting out as he does the good news down the short hall to the back room, where Robert Tagliaferro, he believes, still sleeps.

Robert has been awake since about six, blanket pulled over his head and brooding, day two of the return: July the third, cloudless and exceptionally cool. Ravaged in bowels, lucid in consciousness. In the dark and driving rain, he had seen nothing the night before. Dawn found him staring for many minutes through the office's front windows, waiting for the light and the revelation of the familiar. Except for Joe's, nothing. He'd planned to walk the neighborhood at dawn. No more. The city map cut into the center of his brain, the city directories of recent and ancient vintage, virtually memorized: *basta*. He'll stay in this darkened room forever, and in his mind stroll the streets of east Utica after midnight, a vampire in sunglasses. He'd like to do that. Except for the odors, which would have altered with subcultural alteration. Robert imagines inhaling the differences of absent odors and suffers the assault and battery of nostalgia. How should he lose his sense of smell? Forty-two years of waiting to get back to Utica, properly prepared, in order to get back at Utica. He hadn't imagined that he'd be afraid of Utica. He wanted to come home a stranger and move unseen in the brightness of day among the old faces, all looking exactly as they were, the sounds and the smells, exactly as they were, down familiar streets sauntering unseen, an invisible voyeur, utterly sated. He felt the absurdity of his desire, but it made no difference, except to make him all the more ravenous.

The sovereign ghost lies there curled, under cover. He feels himself fade. Like himself, Utica is unrecognizable except in memory and old photographs.

Door slams, house shakes. Voice of the young man rolls out booming in triumph: "Six percent of seventy thousand is forty-two hundred clams, Mr. Tagliaferro!" Like sudden sunshine, Alex bursts into the darkened room as Robert throws off the blanket, *when we dead awaken,* rises to one elbow, speaks from out of the mood of his morning reverie: "I believe that I am stalking someone, Alex, but I'm not sure who." Alex to the window, throwing up the shade: "You're giving me a headache, Mr. Tagliaferro. *[Pause.]* I got you your house this morning. *[Grins; glows.]* But there's a condition."

"Tell me, what does Sebastian Spina require? That I should present myself to his neighbors as an Algerian refugee, seeking political asylum on Mary Street? I assume that he will not sign unless I agree to impersonate a middle easterner of ambiguous lineage. A possible, but unverifiable nigger. Please, the shade."

"The shade stays up."

"So. He refuses to accept an American thick-lips. Offer him ninety."

"Number one. I didn't make that speech about the nigger moncy. Because I intended to make the deal. If you're in a racial closet, stay in there a few more weeks, because I need the money. Number two. To me *[small smile]* you don't look that much like one."

" 'One' Alex?"

"Just quoting, Mr. T. You enjoy saying that word, let's be frank with each other. Hey! Your lips aren't that thick. Number three. Fuck Spina. Because he didn't make the condition. *[In a high voice:]* 'No commission subtracted?' *[Laps his tongue:]* 'The full seventy for myself?' He's ready to suck our dicks on the nightly news. So I said to Signor Cagato: My client requests an introduction to east Utica's pillars, including yourself. He requires serious involvement and believes that you and you alone can make this happen. When I say 'you and you alone,' he gets his first hard-on in forty years. Then I say, 'Or no deal, goodbye, kiss my ass.'"

"Alex, excuse me. Can it be that you actually talked to him in this spicy manner? Forgive my ingratitude. You're informing me that you made a condition?"

"He drops his pants, bends over and spreads his cheeks. He says, 'Don't bother with the lubricant if you don't want to.'"

"You made a condition for a house that I'm willing to pay an outlandish sum for? Is that what I'm being told in your terrible language?"

"You want goat?"

"Of course."

"In style? In Joe's private cellar? With Our Mother? You said that last night and I respected your wish. *[Pause.]* Last night, you spoke the words 'Our Mother' in public. This is not done in this town. Obviously you know about Our Mother from your research. But he doesn't eat alone, that you didn't know. I've arranged to place you in a circle of people totally psychotic like yourself. These people play the game which I'm guessing you're the master of. Once a week in Joe's cellar, it's Our Mother, it's

Spina, Albert Cesso the twenty-eighth, and my former advisor at
Utica College, Professor Louis Ayoub, the only actual human
being in the group. Always those four, plus Our Mother's best
friend. The game is called Talking Constantly About Utica. I got
us a month of invitations to the weekly funeral. No more books,
Mr. T. You can read the people. That was the condition. Fuck
Spina."

[Pause.]

"Us, Alex?"

"Just like you, I'm a curious man."

"And quite evidently also a psychotic."

"What's two more psychotics to Spina? He tells me it's delicate with Our Mother. He says it's like dealing with a cunt who
never got laid. So he writes a note on our behalf. He tells me to
take the note to the home of Our Mother. He says, 'Follow
instructions all along the line.' He says, 'Our Mother is quite
sensitive. The reactions can be severe.' [Pause.] I saved half of that
fourth cannoli for you. Come on up, I'll make a little lunch."

[Pause.]

"Alex, for lunch I wish for peppers and eggs. [Pause.] Next
week we eat dinner with these people?"

"We don't wait that long. I told Spina that you wanted to
celebrate the Fourth with Our Mother and the boys. I told him
your theme would be Utica and the Founding Fathers. Don't
make a liar out of me, Mr. T. In the cellar, tomorrow night at
eight. I hate Spina."

"And why have you done such great favors for me, Alex?"

"Because your method requires historical understanding of
the living, which you're a little thin on is my guess. I'm the key
to your method. I'm the missing link to the present."

"Alex, toy with me no more. Do you, or do you not, have
in mind peppers and eggs? Don't answer. I request silence. Cook
the peppers first, *al dente,* please, in olive oil and six large cloves
of garlic, so finely sliced with a razor blade that the slivers dissolve

totally in the hot oil. Then scramble in the eggs with light sea-
sonings, very light on the salt, please, and a little sweet basil at the
end, fresh from the garden. Of course, Rintrona's bread, but only
one slice for me, because I do not wish to apply pressure after last
night. And a large pitcher of ice-cold lemonade. In the mode of
Caterina Spina, who means nothing to you, or to the one who
is called Sebastian Spina. In honor of the dead that we love, we
must eat such a meal. Then, for dessert, I'll tell you the story of
in the beginning there was a hole."

—————————⇒·0·⇐—————————

  Just before eight that morning, Alex had driven up to 1303
Mary Street, where he knew, as all east Uticans knew, that he'd
find Sebastian Spina in his blacktopped backyard—Gregorio's garden, shed, and great cherry tree long gone, though not for Alex,
who had never known it any other way. He walks down the
narrow driveway, barely wide enough to accommodate the object
of east Utica's pride and outrage, Spina's late model Mercedes-
Benz, now parked in front of the two-stall garage, with Spina
himself hard at his ablutionary labors, in pajamas, snow boots, a
Yankees' cap, and a plush green tweed sports coat, imported from
Ireland. He's soaping the Mercedes with Ivory dish washing liq-
uid, hosing it down, chamois-wiping it squeaky dry. It occurs to
Alex that Spina is washing his penis prior to coitus. Spina knows
Alex because he knows everyone in east Utica, and because he's
seen the write-ups on the sports page. He's long wanted an
association with this big-shot golfer of local fame, and now the
good Lord has delivered this morsel all of a sudden to my backyard in a golf shirt on this chilly morning. This kid gets so much
pussy he's hot even when it's cold in this cocksucker town, where
summer never comes. Alex, masking himself in politeness, says,
"Good morning, Mr. Spina." Spina, not yet with tongue hanging
out, says, "I've been following you in the paper, my friend, it's an
honor. You're a credit to this town, not to mention the people

of Wales," and then he launches into the high-road rhetoric of his stump speech about "the environmental damage we've undergone in our cities, and in our culture, don't forget our culture, imagine what our lungs must look like, you're a smoker or not regardless, if I find black soot on my car every morning." Having said the words "environmental damage" and "black soot," Spina moves brazenly into the subtext of his campaign for mayor, the racial harassment that he and all the Italians of Utica have been subjected to by the aldermen from the Cornhill district and downtown, "which those people have destroyed, and which I don't have to further analyze for a good-looking person in your line of work. My good friend." The headline on the flyer that his operatives will distribute after the Fourth is to the point: *Uticans Against Further Deterioration of Our Past.* Three years ago, he was himself written up, on the front page, no less, because in debate at a meeting of the Common Council he had thoughtlessly and with no malice whatsoever, so help me God, used the phrase "the Negro element in reference to them, and they have not let up on me since." A week's worth of condescension and contempt poured from the WASP-controlled media, replete with overheated comparisons to bloody black and Italian violence in Brooklyn. It was a gift from God the Father, the birth of his mayoral dream, which would certainly come true in the Fall. The forty or so thousand Italians in Utica were ready, as they had not been for decades, to stand together again at last, and to block-vote Spina to power: to remember, and never again forget, never again, that they were *Italians*, and to say, No more, we will be insulted no more. "We call them blacks, they have to refer to themselves as Negroes. We agree to Negro, they go back to black. These people are breaking my balls, and yours too, my young friend, whether you know it or not, your balls are being broken, don't tell me they're not. And now they imagine themselves to be African-Americans because why? Because they want parity with us. Think about it, my friend. Who in this country goes by the term fill-in-the-blank hyphen American? I mean classically. Who gets media recognition in this country as a fill-in-the-blank hyphen American? Does Dan Rather talk about the Irish-Americans? The Oriental-Americans? The Jew-Americans? Have you ever heard Dan say 'Jew' the way I just said 'Jew,' on the network news at seven o'clock? Pardon me, this is our thing. Mr. Lucas, your background is what, Welsh? *[Alex nods.]* Do you refer to yourself as a Welsh-American? *[Alex shakes his head.]* You have education. You have respect. You don't litter the streets with fast food containers. That's my point. Those people have shit. They like to live in shit. I made my point. We, the Italian-American people of this country, are the original fill-in-the-blank hyphen Americans, we invented that form for ourselves alone. *Sinn fein,* as our Irish brothers say. We Italians are known for our ethnic flare, and now these people want parity? Parity, my ass. And why us is the question I put before you today, pal, and where is their flare? Tell me, where is it? *[Alex smiles.]* Why are we being singled out for a reason they have not yet told us at this time in our tragic history? They don't want equality with the yellow race or the people like yourself who do not hyphenate, and I'll tell you why. These people consider themselves above the Welsh, above the entire WASP element, and all the other coloreds. The arrogance is tremendous. They're above everybody. Except us. This is the bone in their throat. Us. *[Pause.]* Us. *[Pause.]* So they're taking the final racial step. They're saying they have to have equality with the Italian-Americans and then they'll be free at last, thank God almighty, to quote that cunthound they idolize. But I ask you, my friend, how can they be equal? How? *[Alex shrugs and fluffs his balls.]* They're black black black!" Alex says, "I'm going to lift your spirits. I'm going to make you extremely happy, Mr. Spina." Opens his valise. Shows him a document attached to a clipboard. Says, "Read this then sign your name as fast as you can." Spina reads. Spina says, "Fuck me." Reads on. Spina says, "We better go inside." They're at the kitchen table. They have a conversation of some ten minutes which is nothing at all like the one that Alex will report later that morning to Robert. The one valid quotation that he'll pass on has to do with Our Mother, who is indeed likened by Spina unto "a cunt who never got laid." Spina feels bonded. He's never felt that way before. He decides to open up, in all sincerity and honesty. "Remember that movie *Forever Amber*? They're forever black. Is this supposed to be my fault?" Alex replies, "Not in my opinion," and Spina is thrilled: "How can they be equal? The gap is out of this world. When I look at an Arab, what do I see? I grant you, pal, I don't quite see white. But I have to tell you I don't see black either. I know black. There is no color like black. They single us out on the east side because they need to gravitate themselves to the top of the American ladder. Any rung below they consider a slap in the face. These blacks are twisted in their hearts. They have a snobbish mentality, like the English we defeated in the Revolution, but the Italian-Americans of Utica never asked to be put on a pedestal. We did not seek this honor, in this country and what it stands for, one people, indivisible, living in a house divided against itself. *[Spina writes note to Our Mother.]* A familiar situation known to us all in the Caucasian community: You enter a roomful of people where you're not expecting to see one. You go in expecting to have a good time, and then you see one. It's a ton of bricks. What's the first thing that your mind says against your will, because who in his right mind wants to think these thoughts when you're trying to have a good time? Your mind says, A black person is in here. In our very midst. For three minutes your mind is clogged up like a toilet bowl with this thought. If a Chinese walks into a room and sees a black person in there, his mind says the same thing. You ever talk to a Chinese or one of these Mexicans privately about them? Forget the fucking Vietnamese, who've had it up to here. Because why should we lie anymore? All you hear is race race race. I say, okay, let's talk race race race. Black is very very different. And we have the votes. *[Pause.]* We'll destroy them democratically." Alex writes Spina a check for $500. Hands it to him. Spina says,

"What the fuck is this supposed to be?" Alex says, "A promise, Mr. Spina. If Mr. Forza decides to back out for whatever reason, you don't have to give it back. Otherwise, a month from now, assuming the best, I bring you 69,500 in cash." Spina is walking him to the curb. "It is time, my friend, to stop lacerating ourselves at long last for our normal feelings. If you're white, you recoil by nature. So why blame ourselves?" Alex replies, "You tell me." "The white reaction is, Why do I have to look at that? Obviously they feel the same way, but we have the votes. That's it." Alex gets into his car. Spina says: "My signature is worthless, depending on the satisfaction of both parties a month from now. I keep the 500 regardless." Alex says, "You have nothing to fear except fear itself." Neither notices that a few yards away, on the corner of Mary and Bacon, the iron-posted street sign has been yanked up from its footing and is lying on its side in the gutter. The sign itself has been acid-painted. Spina returns to the Mercedes, to wash it again, to soap it down, thinking, An endorsement from this kid would be enormous. In one stroke, the multicultural and the athletic dimension, and then who could screw me? Me, Sebastian Spina.

Alex drives south to the home, just below the Parkway, on upper Mohawk, of the paradoxical Joseph ("Our Mother") Paternostra: slim, spry, ninety years old, and oddly full in the chest. Never called, or referred to, as "Our Mother" within earshot, except once. A major mafia *capo* who had controlled for almost sixty-five years the Utica Syracuse area on behalf of the Don of all of Upstate New York (with the exception of that peculiar toilet: Albany) who resided in Buffalo until he died peacefully two years ago at ninety-four. A struggle for power among younger *capi* had ensued, naturally, one in which Paternostra, it was understood, took no part. Because he had, at his age, earned freedom from such strife; because he had never been suspected of harboring vaulting ambition; because he could no longer command sufficient fire power; because he had grown weary of bloodshed, having in his day, personally, or by order,

executed sixty-four troublemakers. He was just an old man. Each
of the younger *capi* had died violently, in the classic manner. In
Utica, all of the mafia bewitched, and how many there are! assumed that had Paternostra been fifteen years younger, he would
have been anointed by the commission, which could do nothing,
in the absence of a natural inheritor, but watch pointless murder.
Who but Paternostra, after all, had not only a detailed love of
tradition but also such extraordinary rapport with the new generation of *capi*, all of whom had ascended on his voucher? These
dead young *capi*, whose loyalty was sometimes questionable, because they were so selfish and thought only of their so-called
"personal freedom." Was there a smelly phrase that Paternostra
hated more than that one? The philosophy behind it was not
worthy of human beings. Once, he'd referred to them as "indi-
vidualists" to the late Don of Buffalo, and, with ultimate contempt, as our "pro-choice friends." "Yes," the Don had replied,
"they resent our rights over their bodies. Unlike you, Joseph. You,
who are mine."

Alex knocks. A blond, with a modish haircut, a weight-lifter
type, grotesquely muscled, in blue jeans and white sweater, opens
the door and stares brutally. Alex hands him Spina's envelope.
The weight lifter shuts the door. Alex sits on the front stoop and
enjoys the elevated view north, down into the hazy hole of the
heart of the lower east side. Paternostra appears with the blond.
Paternostra in black corduroy Bermuda shorts, white running
shoes, a white sweater, a full head of white hair, more than a trifle
long, a bit wild, like an artist. Alex stands, offers his hand and says,
"Good to finally meet you, Sir. I'm sorry to have interrupted
your morning." Paternostra, looking at Alex happily up and down,
turns to the blond and says, "This handsome youngster has a
natural form, like a god. Nor does he present himself like a
Hollywood hoodlum." Turns to Alex again: "I would be pleased
to see you and your friend at our gatherings. But you must
consult Albert Cesso and Professor Ayoub. First Cesso, who I shall

call. Then the Professor, who I shall not call. It would be criminal. *[Alex smiles; Paternostra is pleased.]* The Professor has veto power. If the Professor vetoes, there is nothing that I can do. *[Pause.]* A person like you, Mr. Lucas, can defy the weather in your golf shirt and we can only be thrilled, even at our age. Good morning, Mr. Lucas. I hope to see you again very soon."

Higher to the Parkway. To Albert Cesso's elegant contemporary home and dental parlors, as he insists on calling them, to the chagrin of local colleagues. Cesso's receptionist buzzes the doctor. He appears, a remarkably shapeless thirty-five-year-old, wearing his ice-blue sanitary gown and the identically hued mask that covers his nose and mouth. Without lifting the mask, he says, "You and your house guest are welcome to join us. I understand from my friend that you may have no dental insurance. My services are yours, whenever you need them, for one dollar per visit, because I shall not insult you with charity. As you speak to the Professor, I will pray to the Virgin to put him into a receptive posture. Hello and goodbye, and may God bless you and keep you, and shine his light upon you." Alex, having said not a word, and with an infinitesimal bow, leaves.

Over to Mohawk again. Down Mohawk into the haze, to Rutger and to Ayoub, Alex's favorite professor, and Alex the Professor's favorite student of all times. Louis Ayoub, fifty-five, professor of fine arts, literature, and philosophy, and avant-garde artist himself, is on the verge of publishing what will be the first and last book of his life. Six months from now he will become Utica's first international literary sensation. The book, bearing the title *The Music of the Inferno,* is a generically unique interweaving of erotic drawings, savage fragments of displaced autobiographical meditation, lyrically soaked fiction, extended analyses of the idea of hell in Western thought (written in the voices of their authors), and gouts of street talk in a twelve-tone scale. Ayoub has been, since his late twenties, when he assumed his position at the college, caretaker of Utica's original fabulous mansion, a stone colossus of eight thousand square feet of living space, heated solely by fireplaces, unfurnished and dank, except in the cozy servant's quarters where, with the woman he's been living in sin with for years, Ayoub sleeps, creates, and cooks occasionally but brilliantly for his only cherished colleagues, Nassar, Cimbalo, and Angelini, which is how he addresses them and everyone he knows, except Alex: surname only, in an impersonally surly tone. As Alex approaches down the long walkway, here they come out of the front door, the happy trio, Nassar, Cimbalo, and Angelini, having just devoured one of Ayoub's obscenely elitist breakfasts, and discussing their prospects for heart attack. They spot Alex, halt, and go deadpan as he reaches them. Alex greets his former teachers. "Alex," says Nassar, "beware. Louis is about to enter his towering rage. At two o'clock this morning he broke through at last to what he calls 'the essential mendacity of Hegel.' He called us to breakfast to give us the news. He was hilarious." Cimbalo says, "Hegel is finished." Angelini says, "And now Louis lies depleted and exhausted. In this mood he can only lash out." Nassar says, "When he's not creating he wants to kill somebody. Whoever comes along." Cimbalo laughs and says, "As you know, Alex, this is normal. Better you than me." "Or me," says Nassar. Angelini looks away, embarrassed. Minutes later, Alex emerges with Ayoub, whose arm is draped around his shoulders. Ayoub says, "I walk along daydreaming as usual and stub my toe. I look down and what do I see? Exactly what I've been looking for all these months in order to complete the final segment of my fantasia. I open the window and a beautiful bird flies in. Tomorrow, at eight, with Forza. Good. I need you both." Ayoub, stratospheric in height, wears a lined raincoat. He weighs in at 254 pounds. He says to Alex, "What are you doing dressed like that? You want to get sick in this weather? Everybody's cold except you."

———⊷•⊶———

They're eating lunch and Robert is drawing out the major innuendoes of Alex's story. "To wit, Joseph Paternostra is responsible for a recent rash of mob hits all over this state. Two in the back of the head. Eight executions must be laid at the door of a ninety-year-old on Mohawk Street. The Godfather of all of Upstate New York, with the exception of Albany, now lives in Utica. I amplify." Alex says, "In my opinion." Robert continues: "Joseph Paternostra was the old Don's catamite, a Queen of the Mafia who gazed lustfully upon you this morning. I amplify."

"What can I say?"

"Albert Cesso is Paternostra's dentist. But Cesso you cannot identify, because he wore a mask. According to you, he has no shape. What we know about Cesso is that he's a religious person. He blesses strangers. But why does a ninety-year-old mafioso befriend a religious dentist? Mysteries abound. Finally, my dear Alex, you tell me that all fear Paternostra, except for Ayoub, whom Paternostra idolizes. As for Spina, I have no choice but to believe you when you tell me that in no time at all he agreed to sell me the ancestral homestead. You are a kind man; on this point you would not prevaricate. But Spina you have surely exaggerated. Please, Alex, please. Contradiction on this point does not become you. I was not born yesterday. You exaggerated. Your hostility toward that pig has produced a language that I regard as unreliable, so distended is it with viciousness and hyperbole." Alex says, "I admit he didn't drop his pants." Robert says, "Thank you. For a moment I thought that I'd stumbled upon a ring of homosexual gangsters."

They've finished lunch. As promised, and without prelude, Robert serves dessert.

"In the beginning, in this valley, on this site, there were a billion of trees, a swamp, a river, and no Indians. Forty miles to the north, a confluence of creeks and streams flowing out of mountains converged to form the original deep black pool, the beginnings of this river that the Indians, who lived on the eastern side of the valley, named after themselves. They called it Mohawk.

We find a livable place, or a river, or a breath-taking mountain, and if it doesn't bear a name we give it our own. We say we discovered it and then promptly puke ourselves upon the landscape. Unlike dogs, we don't mark by urination. We name."

"You promised a different story. In the beginning, there was a hole. Then there was Pellettieri Ave. Tell me that one, Mr. T."

"But I do. At the western edge of this valley, the river they called Mohawk, that had begun far to the north, found its way into the valley at the western edge, into the western door it snuck, spreading itself wider onto the floor of the Mohawk Valley, and it flowed east and south until it encountered elevation, just a half mile north from where we sit, and so it swung about deviously, in a great horseshoe bend, and at the point of maximum curvature, only a few hundred yards, Alex, from where we now sit, it found the lowest place on the valley floor, and there it spread itself very wide, and overflowed in spring thaws and rains, and summer rains and autumn rains, and it made the great swamp, from which issued a stink most horrible, most vile!"

"And they called it Swamp Mohawk, Swimming Hole of our Red-Assed Fathers."

"Imagine the traffic patterns in those times, Alex. The red people followed the easier routes of rivers, not the routes of deer and bear, though they had the legs of Olympic long-distance champions. What cardiovascular systems those red people had! Nevertheless, they did not seek the insane routes of animals, however direct, up and down mountains and through impenetrable densities of thorny bushes, vines, and trees. They walked, they jogged to break up the monotony, on horseback they rode the course of the river, because it was flatter, and smoother, though much longer. Coming from the south along the western edge of the Hudson, and then turning west at the point where the Mohawk obliterates itself at last, rushing into the open arms of the Hudson, they followed the Mohawk west and north, and when they reached the swamp, here, in the center of this territory that the English would call New York, some wanted to go directly north to Canada, but how could they cross the Mohawk unless there was a ford? Forget the canoes. They had to leave the canoes at home. How could they carry forty canoes on an endless journey? For the Hudson, there can be no ford, and there was but one for the Mohawk, and here it was, this was the crossing place for the traffic of the north and the south. Here they stopped a while, and collected themselves out of all the indifferences, and they huddled, and reflected, before crossing this ford. Then they decided. What could be more natural, they agreed, when they came into the stink of this place, then that they should here relieve themselves?"

"They said, Let us now propitiate the Great Anus of Our Fathers."

"It was a gesture of veneration, Alex. Yes. You jest us into the truth. They honored nature in diverse ways. And as their eyes were drawn to the severe north face of the valley, and the mountains beyond, here in this intimate green bowl splashed with yellow flowers, they squatted and they prayed. The red people were deeply religious."

"They said, Let us not embarrass ourselves in the future times by giving this shit hole our name. Let us become the primal polluters. Let us put more shit and piss in it, then let the white people give it their own name. Let them name it, because we're not. And so they squatted and shat, but they did not name this uninhabitable place that became Utica."

"Yes! Utica is the site of the first official rest stop on the original New York State Thruway."

"They arrived. They inhaled. They said, Let us create brown trout, for the future delectation of the white race. They took a dump and called it good."

"Of course, the cause of the stink was a sulfurous spring. Our scientific minds know this."

"But what did those Indians know from sulfur? For that matter, Mr. T, what do you know? You didn't get this from a history book."

"Alessandro Lucca the First, who arrived in Utica in 1850, was Utica's second Italian. Utica's first, John Marchisi, arrived in 1815. Marchisi was told by an Indian of 112 years the primal tale of this city. In a privately published memoir, printed in an edition of three, two of which were destroyed by his bitch beagle, this tale is set down in Marchisi's wretched and virtually incomprehensible English. The sole surviving copy I found buried in the archive of Rutger Bleecker, in the New York Public Library. The archive of Rutger Bleecker himself."

"Rutger Bleecker? That was a person?"

"History, my dear Alex. Everyday you walk and drive on this history. Others spit on it and litter it."

"You read it in a dog-chewed memoir in New York?"

"I alone. And I have returned to tell you all."

Chapter 5

Then this happily failed real estate agent, with yet once more no clients on hand, goes off again into the chilly day, in his short sleeve shirt, to the Valley View Municipal Golf Course, leaving Robert to prepare his entrance for the Fourth of July. His theme: "Utica and the Founding Fathers": Because Alex had obligated him. The long rehearsal of his life is over. Time to give the audience his gifts of history. Down their throats.

Except for a review of the notes that he'd virtually memorized, he wouldn't need to prepare the moment. What he wanted to prepare was his appearance. The horror that he saw in the mirror. What would they think of his awful clothes? But what, at sixty, could he do about his appearance? What would he be willing to give to look again like the young man he used to be? Who, as a young man, felt himself to be so repugnant. Hopeless.

Alex returns to find Robert in the front office, sitting with his feet up on the desk, in a familiar pair of blue jeans, a long-sleeved white shirt, a yellow tie whose narrowness marks it as forty years out of date, and Melvina's almost perfectly preserved white watch cap. Before Alex can speak, sensing that Alex is about to speak, Robert jumps in: "Master Alessandro, what is wrong? Did you golf badly today? In this smoky valley, many find themselves chained to a burning gulf."

[Alex turns away. To window. Back to Robert.]

"Who said you could wear the pants?"

"Such a voice!"

[Back still to Robert. Small but significant increase in volume.]

"I said who said?"

"No one said. Surely you toy with me. These are but old pants."

[Alex turns to Robert. Very quiet. Toneless.]

"You rummaged."

"I was only looking to hang my few things. I opened the hall closet and found it stacked with boxes, through which I refused to rummage. Naturally, I felt a powerful urge. Alex, for forty-two years I have rummaged and foraged through times past, patching myself as I read. Then I saw them hanging at the far right end and I could not resist. I said to myself, 'Those are jeans from Alex's early teens, the pre-robust years, which he saves because he is a secret sentimentalist.' On me look how they fit with flare! *[Looks down at self.]* Alex! Your teenage years are in me reborn and now I contemplate calling a young lady, upon whom I gazed from afar in my senior year at Proctor High. Geraldine, who broke my heart. The husband, a drunken, vainglorious lout, is dead."

"Get those pants off."

"Alex—"

"Off."

"You speak like an angry corpse."

"They're not mine."

[Pause.]

"Alas, poor fellow."

[Alex stares.]

"These jeans are your wife's. You have no pictures, but you kept the clothes. After three months of pregnancy, the beautiful Caroline Lucas could not wear these jeans. And she never wore them again. Now you recall in me the end of the first trimester, when Caroline lost her form, and you lost the woman you knew. I speculate."

[Alex, back again to Robert. Silence.]

"Alex?"

"I don't care."

"That I speculate?"

[Pause.]

"Let's drop it."

"What is it that you wish to drop?"

"Nothing."

"The nothing that is?"

"If you need to wear the pants, go ahead. Wear the pants."

"You don't object?"

"I'd prefer not to."

[Pause.]

"I saw the pants; I saw you as a boy. They made me feel contemporary. They made me feel . . . I can't find the word."

"Svelte."

"Yes! In the English Renaissance, this word was unknown."

"It's not my word."

[Pause.]

"I think I know whose word it was. Can you read my thoughts?"

"Forget it."

"Alex's theme. Our unhappy relation to the past."

"Your tie is ridiculous."

"But yours would be a la mode. Perhaps you will allow me to wear one of yours?"

[Alex turns to Robert. Points, theatrically.]

"The hat."

"I wore it when I was last in Utica."

"The hat is sensational. Except for that rusty spot."

"It's blood. Blood of the innocent. A remembrance of my last hunt in this horrid valley."

"Only one."

"Alex?"

"One tie. I have only one. One expensive tie."

"I don't doubt it."

"Handmade in Italy out of pure silk. Royal blue tulips printed on ecru and navy checks. One hundred and ten clams."

"It would be an honor."

[Pause.]

"The tie is superb."

"This shirt is not superb, but it's mine. These pants are your wife's, and they have lifted my spirits. This hat was made for me long ago by my stepmother. If we could only add your extraordinary tie, I would qualify as the fool, in modern motley all clad."

"I'll be right back."

Alex returns with tie. Robert says, "I shall tie on the tie." Alex says, "Tie on your cravat." Robert says, "A French loan word must be used sparingly, if at all." Ties it on. Alex steps back and says, "Hey! You intend to shave?" Robert says, "No." Alex says, "Good. By tomorrow night, you'll be Robert a la mode. But I'm warning you. When you eat, especially the way you eat, watch out. Do not contaminate the cravat. Now put that jacket on, or I'll get angry."

[Robert dons ancient blue blazer.]

"How do you feel? Feel good?"

"I'll know how I feel when I'm in the cellar tomorrow night."

⇒•◄

Robert asks about the sirens that he'd heard all night long, and Alex responds by inviting him to watch the eleven o'clock evening news. At about ten, Alex hears Robert's voice in urgent one-way conversation. The old guy is on the phone with the widow! As quietly as he can, he climbs down the back stairs and enters the front office to find it empty, and the conversation still in progress, in Robert's room, where there is no phone. Alex walks with deliberate heaviness down the short hall to find him sitting, an invisible phone to his ear, saying, "But Geraldine." Robert does not see Alex; he's taking in Geraldine's response, right hand over his heart. "Geraldine," he says, hunched over a little, eyes downcast, "all these years you've come to me in dreams." Looks up. Freezes in position. Speaks, without a trace of embarrassment: "Alex, I believe that it would go better if I actually wrote the script. A person like yourself, of course, would never need to do such a thing. *[Phone disappears.]* I'm not a person like yourself. Would you help me with my script?" Alex wants to know what Robert means by referring to him as a "person like yourself." "Outside the fact that I'm a little younger." Robert tells him that he, Alex, "cuts quite a figure, in the great world beyond these rooms, apart from one's private opinion of you." He tells Alex that, "for example," a young lady "who claims to know you," had stopped by twice this after-noon, "while you were enjoying yourself on the links." Alex wants to know what she looked like and Robert tells him "like a vision," then proceeds to describe a beauty resembling Caroline Lucas not at all. Alex sits in the other chair, the wingbacked one. Reaches up with both hands, grasping the top edges of the wings. A muscular pose, yet relaxed, and a little amused: wings on wings. He wants to know what she had to say, "in detail." Robert tells him, with a shrug, "some matter of a rental property." The details escape him, he wasn't interested in the details, because the "subtext, as I grasp it, was not commercial. It was romantic." Robert says, "Obviously you know her and resist. She will defy your celibacy, this is a certainty. And this too you know. But do you know that she will succeed?" Alex says, "I'm thinking about it." Robert says, "The pronoun reference is vague." Alex says, "Her eventual success."

"Alex, how does a young man restrain his passion?"

"His what?"

"How does an old man rekindle his?"

"By following my instructions. Ready?"

"I fear not."

"Stand."

[Robert stands.]

"Follow me."

[They walk down short hall to office.]

"Sit there."

[Robert sits at desk.]

"What is this, Robert?"

"A telephone."

"An actual telephone."

"I'm not ready."

"Good. That's the essence of it."

"The pronoun reference is vague."

"No books, no notes."

"A one page outline?"

"No outline. Leap into the dark. That's how you rekindle."

"My hands. Look at these hands, Alex."

"They're not that bad."

"But they're bad."

"Yes. They're bad. But she'll be partially swept away by the jeans and the tie."

"Ah, partially."

"Best to go in with brutal self-awareness. She won't be blind to the hands."

"Then she will love me for the damages I have sustained, and I will love her that she does pity them."

"Eventually, down the road, she loves the hands."

"Future tense."

"It takes time. Call."

"You call first."

"Geraldine wouldn't go for me."

"Do you require more time to reflect?"

"On what?"

"Your outline! To approach Heather."

"You're on a first name basis with her?"

"Call Heather now. I will listen. I will take notes for my script. Then I'll call Geraldine. After that, it will be time for the late news. This lady of yours is beautiful. She is educated. You please her greatly. She is alive, Alex. She is sunshine itself. This is such a personality that it will pull you from your grave. You, who are half in love with easeful death."

"Forget Geraldine totally. You fell for Heather."

"No, Geraldine is the one for me."

"The last time you saw this chick you were what? Eighteen?"

"Oh, God, Alex. What a falling off there must have been."

"Good."

"Good!?"

"You'll be neck 'n' neck with her, in the home stretch, going down to the wire."

"Alex, it's cruel to remind your elders of the nearness of death. Geraldine and I do not require this reminder 'Going down to the wire.' We don't like the metaphor. If I may speak for Geraldine, at this juncture in our relationship."

"Robert. Neck 'n' neck together again at last. Going down together. Think about it."

"Caroline went down. You stayed up here. Heather arrived. This is what I'm thinking about."

"Heather."

"Heather will please you greatly."

———

Robert asks, "What time is it?" Alex answers, "Quarter of." Robert says, "Time enough, I think." He dials from memory. A silence. Hangs up and says, "No longer in service. Strange." Checks

phone directory and can find no listing for a Geraldine Paladino.
Turns, puzzled, to Alex. About to speak when he understands the
mistake. He had taken the number from the Utica city directory
at the New York Public, not the current telephone directory. He's
two years out of date. Dials information and is told that there is
no such listing. An unlisted number? No. Returns to phone directory to take down the number of the one Paladino listed.
Remo Paladino, the younger brother. Calls. Awkward introduction, then a silence. Repeats the introduction, this time even
more awkwardly. A silence. "Well, the reason I call, as I've just
twice stated, is that as an old and cherished friend of your incomparable sister's I wonder if—." Long silence. "I see." Brief silence.
"I wonder if you would be so kind—." Brief silence. "Kind, yes.
I said that word. Would you be so kind as to tell me where I might
find her." Brief silence. "Find. I'm sorry. A manner of speaking,
Remo." Brief silence. "Thank you very much, Remo." Hangs up
and turns to Alex, who asks, "Where does Remo say she can be
found?" Robert replies: "She can be found at the Forest Hill
Cemetery. That is what Remo says. Let's watch the news."

——➤•◄——

They're in Alex's small front parlor watching Ross DiStefano,
Kathleen Krocker, and, at the sports desk, Nick LeoGrande, who
leads off the hour with a promise to tell viewers of his "revealing
encounter" with "recently crowned upstate amateur golf king,
Utica's own Alex Lucas." Ross and Kathleen follow with stiff-
jawed intonations of the headlines: "Another week of fireworks,
Kathleen. What will the Fourth of July bring?" "Seventeen blazes
of suspicious origin, Ross, since the first of the year." "Plus the
developing mystery of the street signs, right after these messages
from our sponsors."
    Alex hits the mute button on the remote. Robert says, "I
remember a detail." Alex looks at Robert. Robert says, "When
she left, she said to mention to you that she never played. The

game as such never held interest. But she carried her father's clubs
as a youngster. She said, 'Tell him I'm an experienced caddy.' No,
you misunderstand, Alex. Heather is fearless, but not bold. She
would not intrude. And she respects herself. In my opinion, you
give signs." Alex brings back the sound. Ross is talking about last
night's fires. "Utica is ablaze again . . . Rutger, Oneida . . . the
Cornhill district." Robert asks Alex to kill the sound. He says, "As
I suspected. But I did not know that there had been so many.
And that, too, is the history of this city. Tomorrow night, in the
cellar, 'Utica and the Founding Fathers' will not be heard. Our
theme will be fire. Our theme is fire. She would not intrude, Alex.
She knows what she wants, but she is discreet and composed, not
to mention the warmth, the openness, the beauty. You give obvious
signs. Heather knows this. I know this. I believe in Heather. I
believe that you do not know. In her presence, you relax. I speculate. You enter another context. You focus. You come into the world
of sun. You do this, but you do not know that you do this. Pure
speculation. You do not know that you are happy in her context.
Her offer to caddy is a response to your response. But you do not
know that you have responded. A state that has much to recommend it. A blessed state, in a way. How long have you known her?"

"Six months. I handle her rental properties."

"A woman of means?"

Alex brings back the sound. Interviews with city officials
about "the alleged arson crisis of recent months, Ross." Robert
says "please." Silence again. Robert says, "The grave's a fine and
private place." Alex picks up his cue: "But none, I think, do there
embrace." Robert says, "Ayoub's poetry class?" Alex says, "She
won't talk me into it." Robert says, "I believe that in her presence
you achieve incarnation. You return to the earth. In my opinion,
your daughter needs her father. Excuse me, Alex, life's worst
stupidity is what they call beating around the bush. Your daughter
will need to know that you kept the jeans. We don't have time,
not even at your age. Let's not be stupid."

Alex brings back the sound. Interview with "soon-to-be-declared mayoral candidate, Alderman Sebastian Spina," who claims that the fires and the street sign incidents are linked. "Our heritage and our very identity as Americans suffer under this siege, my fellow Uticans." Robert is transfixed by Kathleen's description of the street-sign incidents. Twenty-four in two months. All but the first in east Utica. Uprooted and acid-painted. Urine traces not canine. Robert says, "The stupid Spina pours venom, of course, but nevertheless he has struck deep. His oratory in spite of itself bears insight of shattering force. Please, Alex, the sound." Alex hits mute and says, "You want to meet a woman?" Robert says, "I want to meet Geraldine." Alex says, "Want to hear something funny?" Brings back the sound: Nick LeoGrande saying that he spotted Alex at Valley View this afternoon. That he requested an interview. That Alex told him "no interview," but he'd give a quote. "Alex Lucas is retiring from competitive golf. A tremendous shock, folks." Nick, sad-faced, is saying, "An athlete cut off tragically in his prime, by his own hand." Ross says, "Goodnight, Kathleen." Kathleen says, "And while the blazes rage on, goodnight Ross, goodnight Nick, and from all of us to all of you, goodnight Utica."

Soundlessly, Robert weeps. Stands. Alex cannot respond. Were he to be asked, "Why do you weep, Robert?" he would respond, "In truth, I do not know."

Robert requests a key to the front door. Alex cannot rise from his chair. Robert is going for a walk. Alex finally speaks: "At this hour?" Robert says: "To meet the long-familiar dead."

Chapter 6

He hears the door. Rises and goes to the front window to gaze down on the man in the white watch cap, the man in Caroline's jeans, passing through the illuminated area of the street lamp, heading north on Pellettieri Ave. Then just the white cap catching light in the blackness. He's gone. And Alex wants to. How shall he make love to a ghost? Louis Ayoub had taught him how. Taught him the word: *Liebestod.* Played the recording. Said, in response to his incredulity: "Alex, the happiest of conjunctions." Come, and die. Isolde, sipping the heavenly fragrance, plunging beneath the voluptuous swell and riding down into her bliss. Love-death. But Isolde had the warm body of Tristan before her. What shall Alex do for a warm body? Ayoub had given him only an idea, and an example, from the rare world of art. It was LeoGrande, unwittingly, who had taught him how. "Tragically," said the prescient sportscaster, "by his own hand."

On the way out, he took Alex's sunglasses and a large manila envelope, thick with notes on the history of his surname. Walked two blocks north on Pellettieri Ave, to Broad, because he needed to avoid Catherine and Bleecker, the safer and more direct routes. Then east toward a tenement on Catherine Street, one block north of Bleecker. He would find Broad dark and inhuman with abandoned industrial buildings of endless length and scores of broken windows, and a few businesses, current and intact, but at this hour also dark. Scaglione Prosthetics. Auto Damage Appraisers. Utica Spray and Chemical. Big Anthony's Crane, Forklift, and Demolition. And the vacant lots of trash. On Broad, no conversations afloat in backyards under grape trellises. No backyards. No family-run markets. No stogies glowing in the dark. No families. Nothing that is not there, fingering his memory. Only fast traffic. He would find Broad kind.

<hr />

He touches himself. Unzips his fly. Puts his hand in. Alex needs to. Takes hand out. Leaves fly unzipped. Unbidden, an aphorism from his early teens: When in doubt, whip it out. He's certainly in doubt. He wanted to talk back to Louis Ayoub. Tell him were it Tristan singing at the end over Isolde's body, he, Tristan, could whip it out, and come on her body. In his death, all over her death. But he, Alex, is Tristan in an empty house. Alex has a thought. Goes downstairs to the hall closet stuffed with her boxes. So many unmarked boxes. So much desire. Which is the one of her toiletries, where he had also stored her bedtime apparel? He wants to locate it by smell. Gets down among the boxes, nosing, a dog with a hard-on, trying to catch a whiff of a bitch in heat, four miles away. Hand back in. Hand so full. Lips parted, sniffing among the boxes. No use. One by one, drags them into the hallway, all impatient in his passion and spilling out the contents, he'd spill himself out soon all over her things, the hall a chaos of everything he'd hidden for two years. There it is. Puts hand in and takes out penis. Erect. Wants to now. Hesitates. Because he has another thought. Does not bother to put it back in. Fully clothed, with an erect penis leading the way.

======>-0-<======

He stands before a darkened tenement on Catherine Street. Removes sunglasses. Knows that he shouldn't wake the old man at this hour. But the dead are not considerate. He knocks. Nothing. Etcetera, for several minutes, increasing the force as the minutes drag on. Now he's pounding on the door, because the dead are not gentle, and he hears a voice garbled behind the pounding. Stops. The voice again: "Who are you?" Robert says, "Uncle Morris, it's me, Robert." Without hesitation, with no trace of alarm, the voice replies: "Give me a minute." More than a minute passes. Footsteps to door. Key in lock. Footsteps away from door. The voice, calmly: "Come in, Robert." Robert turns the knob and steps into an intense beam of light, trained on his face. All else in pitch dark. The beam is attached to twin barrels, perhaps of a shotgun, pointed at him. The intense light, the twin barrels: that's all that he can see. He can only assume a shotgun hoisted against the shoulder of the man who said, "Come in, Robert," the man he believes to be Morris Reed. Robert says, "Uncle Morris." The voice says, "Shut up." Robert says, "Uncle Morris, it's only me." The voice says, "Don't call me Uncle Morris. I need to kill you." Robert says, "Please." The voice says, "Your face has become as ugly as your soul. Now pray to the Lord." Robert has a thought: "Is that Gregorio's shotgun?" The voice says, "Maybe so." Robert says, "The ammunition that I left?" The voice says, "Maybe so." Robert says, "Forty-two years ago?" The voice says, "Take your head off just like the new stuff." Robert says, "It's defunct." The voice says, "Then you won't mind what I have to do now, which is put your brains on the wall." Robert hits the floor. The flashlight, a hefty one, is slammed down hard on the back of one hand, then the other. On the fingers: the flashlight wielder in-

tending to produce maximum pain, not knowing Robert's peculiar immunity. No screams. The voice, in bitterness: "So you are
dead, after all. Too bad. I was hoping to make you holler and cry the
way we did all those years." Lights. Robert on his belly, face resting
on the thick envelope, broken open, some of its contents spilled out.
Morris says: "You vomit the paper? Wouldn't surprise me."

<hr/>

He's in the bathroom of the gargoyle-footed tub, where he'd
felt himself lured, so many times, to observe her at her bath. He
sitting on the one place available: the toilet. To observe, to converse, to play the game. Shall he go to her in the tub, partially
clothed, crazy with his shoes still on, or will she come out to
make love to him on the floor? Or do they hold off, and race
upstairs, hotter than ever, Alex unbuckling as they go? On the
stairs? In the kitchen? Do they make it to the bedroom? In
conversation on the things of the day, as she soaped and massaged,
the suddenness of erotic surprise, the discontinuity, the conversa-
tional leap itself erotic: sometimes as she shaved her legs in oiled
waters. "You want to fuck me, Alex?"

He's running the bath. Following her routine: Epsom salts, so
soothing for muscular aches, "I'm aching for your muscle, Alex,"
and a splash of olive oil, "to soften and lubricate my Irish skin."
"Take off your shirt. No. Just the shirt." He's naked, easing down
into the hot bath, worrying that he might spoil it. Come too
soon in the oiled water, he's soaping and massaging, he's oiled and
lemon-scented, surrounded by her night things: the creams, the T-
shirts, the lotions, the running shorts arranged all around the tub.
"These are my creams, Alex." The final photo taped to the mirror. On the floor, within easy reach, the safety razor with which
she shaved her legs. He remembers, absurdly, a literary game that
he played as a teenager. Invented authors and titles combined for
obscene effect. Tumescent in the tub, this is what he remembers:
Mutilation in Moscow, by Ivan Cutchercockoff. He grins. His erec-

tion falls off, some. Good. He won't come too soon. Picks up razor, lifts a leg, as she did, points strongly through the toes, as she did, a balletic effect, and he feels graceful, he senses that he has achieved a formal moment, a kind of release, pointing strongly through the toes, and this brawny ballerino begins to shave his legs, concentrating fiercely, pointing strongly, "your cock is swelling again," afloat on the oiled water, "My swell Alex."

The photo taped to the mirror, in sumptuous color. An eight-by-ten blow up. At the bottom, and lower right hand side, a baby's head, shoulders (surprisingly broad), chest. Mouth wide open, screaming and cavernous, like an opera singer in the climactic scene. The baby is blood-smeared, as are the latex gloved hands holding her, which belong to the delivery doctor, not otherwise visible. Occupying the left hand side, a nurse, partially visible, looking down at what is not fully visible: the naked lower half of the mother. In retrospect, we say that the nurse bears awareness of the inaugural moment of uncontrollable hemorrhage. The doctor has just cut the umbilical cord and is about to place the baby at the mother's breast, where she will commence to suck superbly. The nurse wants to say, "Doctor, —" but stifles herself, because bleeding at the inaugural moment of fatal discharge is not distinguishable from normal post-partum discharge. Blood on the baby, on the doctor's hands and gown, on the floor. Blood is present. Prescience is not present. Father and medical personnel about to take delight in the baby's advanced sucking power, for a moment. Medical personnel, including a second nurse, not visible and smiling at the father, alert and exceptionally qualified. The woman at the center of the photo looks into the camera after almost fourteen hours of labor. Her breasts spill from the hospital gown. Nipples erect. Trying to smile (we say in retrospect), but the mouth has refused and turned itself down into the grief of happiness. She is ruined and she is happy. In no other photo of her in his possession do her cheek bones seem so to protrude, as if they've moved forward, stretching the flesh gaunt behind them, hollowing out the cheeks. The eyes are glassed, vacant. In retrospect, we see the vacancy as terror, but she is not terrified. She is happy. Most of all: an effect of frozen motion, like Michelangelo, it pleases us to think so, a yearning expressed as a straining toward the man behind the camera, as if head and shoulders would lift and twist toward him. This woman is depleted, and a few minutes from her final oblivion.

The man in the tub, shaving his legs, is in a panic. Without having touched or stroked it since lowering himself into the water—she called it his cock, always, his cock, it's reached the edge of orgasm, all by itself. He's not ready. He will not finish the second leg. Turns on hot water. Lies back. Removes blade from razor. At the instant of orgasm, this Tristan would sever the root of his passion, at the root.

—⇒•⇐—

They sit across from one another in the small living room. Robert in sunglasses again. With the manila envelope in his lap, Morris the shotgun in his. Robert asks him to put the shotgun away. Morris refuses. Morris says, "We thought you were kidnapped and murdered. The police paid no attention to the grieving niggers. Why did you leave us?" Robert says, "I don't know for certain." Morris hoists the gun to his shoulder and says, "I'll help you to know for certain." Robert says, "Uncle Morris, of that I'm sure, you are not capable." Morris puts the gun down on the floor. There are tears in his eyes. He says, "You disgust me. Not a word for forty-two years. How could you do such a thing to us?" Robert says, "I wasn't trying to do harm." Morris says, "When you were little, and couldn't pronounce 'l,' you called this the weaving room. For years after, your aunt and I called it the weaving room. Do you remember?" Robert says, "No." Morris says, "We were good to you. Do you deny that?" Robert says, "No. I do not deny it. Nor do I affirm it. My memory of the years with you and Aunt Melvina is cloudy. I must assume decency. You are good people."

"You never loved us, did you?"

"I lived here. I was taken care of. In retrospect, I'm grateful to you both. When did she die?"

"You don't deserve to know. I'll never tell you."

"I recollect one distinct feeling. I was never comfortable. I was nobody's child. Can you deny it?"

"We couldn't hide you in our name, because you didn't look black enough for us to give you our name. But look at you now. You turned white at last. Ugly and white."

"I bought Gregorio's house, Uncle Morris."

"Will you find your comfort there?"

"No."

"You vicious bastard."

Silence.

"Why live there then? Because you wanted to be an Italian? Is that it? Because you have one of those infernal names?"

"Yes."

"Yes, what?"

"I have one of those infernal names."

"They treated you well at that house, didn't they?"

"Yes."

"Better than we did?"

"They were old. They had no responsibilities toward me."

"Was there a law that said they had to be kind to you?"

"They made a fuss. It was easy for them to be kind."

"Nothing was easy for us, Robert. We worked hard."

"Uncle Morris, please."

"Shut up. Sometimes second jobs because we were saving up for your college, like I've been saving up for this speech. We gave you healthy food. We bought too many toys. Changed your shitty diapers. We were scared to death when you were sick with the ordinary illnesses of children. I watched you sleep in your crib all night a hundred times because I was afraid you'd stop breathing.

Too bad you didn't. We played with you, you mean bastard. We said 'No' when you would do a thing that would hurt yourself. We danced around the kitchen with you to the radio music, and you constantly demanded that certain songs be repeated, but we couldn't make the radio do that, and it grieved us. Do you remember? We kept the house clean. We let you have too much ice cream. Try to remember."

"You couldn't have your own, Uncle Morris."

"You were our own, you vicious bastard."

"I am certainly a bastard."

"So what?"

"I had nobody to call father."

"You had me. You had Melvina. And you threw us away, like garbage. Now you come back to tell me that you cannot remember how we loved you so much. You do not remember. Not even one letter. You do not remember because you are evil. The evil ones have no memory."

"I have no memory of my father. In the absence of my father, I acquired knowledge. My knowledge is my memory."

"Does your knowledge love and care for you?"

"Did my father?"

"You son of a bitch. Try to remember."

"I thought of you as kind strangers. Instead of a father, I have knowledge."

"To make up for the pain of your boyhood, when we were loving you."

"Where was I born?"

"My memory is cloudy."

[Pause.]

"Nothing can ease the pain of my boyhood. I was an ethnic freak in this fair city of such clear ethnic divisions. I have come back to return the pain."

"You are returning the pain."

"I did not intend to hurt you, Uncle Morris."

"What's in that envelope?"

"Nothing, Uncle Morris."

"Something is in there. You brought it here to show me."

"Nothing, Uncle Morris. In truth, nothing."

"Stop calling me Uncle Morris. The way you talk, you're an iceberg."

<hr>

He can't retrieve Caroline. In his erotic abandon, it's Heather he sees, and he's giggling, *Cutchercockoff.* Will the flood of his semen actually raise the water level? It's over. He decides to finish shaving the second leg. "How ripe, how golden are your thighs, Alex." Pointing strongly through the toes.

He says out loud, "You want to fuck me, Heather?" The sound of the words, so strong and delicious, make him want to again—beneath the voluptuous swell.

The Fourth of July

R obert says, "My entrance, Alex. My entrance," and Alex, with Heather-induced jauntiness, promptly takes his assigned place at the front window of the realty office, to begin the watch. Here they come: On a bicycle, Ayoub in racer's goggles, helmeted, raincoat streaming and whipping behind him. Alex sings out: "The Thinker, as it were." On foot: Paternostra with uplifted gaze, in a black double-breasted Italian suit, by Giorgio Armani (courtesy of Giorgio Armani), accompanied by the blond weight lifter, pavement-gazing in gray sweat clothes, carrying a grocery bag which contains an apron, a chef's hat, and a revolver. Like Italian men of an older generation, they walk arm in arm, the downcast blond assuming the male role. They have not, over the entire journey, spoken a word. As Paternostra clutches the proffered arm of his friend, as Joe's comes into view, something surges up inside of him. Paternostra needs to be swallowed whole by this moment, to be gathered bodily into eternity. He would speak now. Pour something out. Nothing pours. He only says, "Raymond." His tone requires no response, and Raymond gives none. With a little bit of confidence, Alex says, "The Killers." And now by taxi Albert Cesso, whose frontside, from the neck all the way down, were he to be seen in the nude, would be difficult to distinguish from his backside, all the way down. Cesso wears an aqua leisure suit, circa 1975, the top three buttons of his flowered white shirt undone, revealing a flashing silver crucifix, nested in the exceptional density of his black chest hair. Alex says, "Heigh-ho! The Masked Man! Unmasked, I think." And finally Spina, all puffed out in his Mercedes, Spina parking it so piggishly, aslant three spaces in Joe's lot, besuited in pinstripes against a charcoal background, bought in 1968, when he had seen on television, that grievous summer, exactly so besuited, the elegant mayor of New York, that tall and handsome liberal, that cocksucker, John Lindsay. Shoulders hunched, hands rammed in pockets, shivering in the cold, Spina trots into Joe's, as Alex chants: "Mr. Rab-BIT is HERE with the SHIT!" He pauses. Then says: "You're on, Mr. T."

Robert pulls his blazer by the back of its collar, up and over his head, down over his face: Alex's cue to usher him out and across the street, like a detective transporting a criminal suddenly gone shy before the cameras, our golf-shirted athlete, who never shivers, bundling into Joe's this hooded phantom and choosing not to enter through the convenient door that opens into the dining room. Not in order to spare the diners his dreadful companion—those slummers from the suburbs, those scowling families, ex-Italians all, seeking contact with their roots. Spare them? Alex? He takes Robert, instead, through the bar entrance, because a trap door is located there, behind the bar: the only way into the cellar.

He's Big John, the owner and bartender, alerted by Paternostra that there would be two new guests this evening, one of whom would be Alex Lucas, his famous neighbor, and they were to be granted freedom of the cellar. But this? What is this? Big John feels crushed beneath a ton of disgust. Had he not inserted his finger into the dike for two decades or more? Christ, there were times when he'd put his entire fist in there. The earrings. The nose rings. The cunt rings. The baggy pants. The circus of freaks who walk our streets. Why has a nice, clean-cut golfer, who eats here twice a week, regardless, chosen to insult me with this spectacle? Why should I, of all people, in my own establishment, have to take it up the ass?

The laughers and the loudmouths and the lonely men go silent and stare. John snatches from his trophy shelf, from the shrine to Saint Mickey, the mighty bat autographed by the mighty man himself, and says: "You disappoint me, Alex."

Alex says, "John."

John says, "You're breaking my heart."

The hood says, "This rough Ahab would strike through the appalling wall of my identity."

Robert unveils himself.

"Take him down before I kick him down."

And down, down they go, deep into Joe's bowels, into the silence, descending with their backs to the welcoming party, the five respectful men who stand at the table. Halfway down and already he feels awash in shitty ordinariness, a little depressed, because this is not the setting he'd imagined, but this is nevertheless Robert's theater: Two naked bulbs for lighting, cardboard cases stacked and strewn, a coal bin and a shovel, a dolly, a formerly white refrigerator, and a space heater working at low power against the cool dampness. Odor of dust, ambiance of gray, and in dramatic relief: The vivid and hearty men who await them. He's down, he turns and sees them at the large round rough-hewn table, in a space shockingly foreshortened (behind the table) by two floor-to-ceiling ovens stretching from side wall to side wall, eating up three-quarters of the cellar. There is so little room. The vivid bodies are so close. Whitish Robert whitens. Introductions, hand shakes, deeper silence, broken at last by Paternostra, who says, "Sit where you please, Mr. Forza. Our circle permits no hierarchy, nor do we wish for one. Mr. Lucas, this chair, I believe, bears your name": with a pleasant face, pointing to the chair next to his own. Robert, expressionless, actually ignoring Paternostra, turns to Alex, who's already moving to the chair that bears his name. Robert says: "Goat meat is fairly firm, with a pleasant flavor, but a strong smell, quite disagreeable if taken from the adult. Have I lost my sense of smell, Alex? Is it to be hot dogs?"

Cesso, guiding Robert gently, hand on his back, to a chair beside his: "Oh, yes! And hamburgers and chips! Corn on the cob, Mr. Forza. Today we honor America. With gratitude in advance, I propose a toast to Mr. Forza for the lecture that he has promised us on our patriotic past."

Raymond pours wine all around.

Cesso: "To Mr. Forza and our Founding Fathers."

All drink, except Robert, who says, "Our Foundering Fathers," in response to which Ayoub, who's beginning to smell a rival, flourishes his wit: "And their Foundling Sons."

Robert raises his glass and replies: "Stand up for bastards!"

Then Spina, needing to establish himself to the newcomer: "I guess we got your goat, my friend."

Spina guffaws.

Silence.

Robert replies, "Am I your friend, or am I your benefactor? If the latter, never the former."

Cesso: "Be kind, Muzzy," using the hated nickname of Spina's childhood and teen years, a name from which he'd hidden since the beginning of his political career, but the name which these men occasionally deployed in order to prick his bloated presence. Spina has been pricked. Pleasure in the cellar, but puzzlement too. This Forza had made a covert declaration. Spina, clearly, belongs to him. Raymond opens the oven door and removes a grill of sizzling dogs and burgers. Places on a clean grill the untoasted buns. Spina forks a dog; Cesso says, "Muzzy." Spina returns the dog.

Paternostra says, "Raymond will arrange your desire for goat, as a surprise, in the near future."

Robert says, "And I will arrange a surprise for you, sir, perhaps this very evening."

Raymond turns to the oven, ostensibly to remove the buns, and does remove the buns, but not before adjusting something beneath the apron and sweat pants. In the sudden silence, the space heater's drone dominates.

Alex, who's caught Raymond's move, says to Paternostra, "That heater, Mr. Paternostra."

"Yes, Alex?"

"Is it necessary?"

Ayoub, who's been eyeing Robert, decides to fish for vulnerability: "Raymond, the last time you cooked the meal in question, how many kids did you slaughter?"

"On the average four, depending."

"Depending on what, Raymond? Show consideration to our

guests, who have not been privy to our understanding. Spit it out Raymond, for the gentle guests."

"Depending on the size of the kids. Depending on what you tell me the night before. You call and tell me how hungry you forecast yourself. Three or four, sometimes five, depending on your forecast and the size."

Ayoub: "Alex, you appear to have suddenly lost your magnificent tan. My dear Alex, did you think that we consumed the adult animal? So wrinkled and so leathery? We don't eat smelly old goat. *Capretto,* Alex. Who eats an old goat? Tell us, Raymond. Spit it out."

Paternostra, serenely: "Old goat is an acquired taste, Professor, as Raymond knows. My Raymond never spits it out. My deep friend, Raymond, is a discreet connoisseur."

Cesso blushes.

Ayoub bores in: "Raymond, how does one acquire goat in Utica and its verdant environs? At which supermarket?"

"You going to break my balls all night with that teacher voice?"

"Your balls, Raymond? You believe I've touched your balls? Albert, tell our good guests how many kids you've brought into our Mohawk Vale of tears. Do not include the Vietnamese adoption."

Cesso, into his plate: "I include him, Louis."

Paternostra, with a little pain: "Professor, with all due respect."

Ayoub: "Did you say 'respect,' Joseph?"

Paternostra: "I do not excuse Raymond's language and I do not follow your course."

Alex, the eager student: "I've been in Raymond's shoes. I've seen the Professor in action. It's the conceit! In my opinion, he's teaching the conceit by performing one."

Robert: "The yoking together, by violence, of widely disparate ideas, in truth radically similar."

Spina: "Hey! Hey! LBJ! How many kids did you kill today?"

Robert: "Mr. Spina, touché."

Paternostra: "Mr. Lucas, you are not similar to Raymond. You have not been in Raymond's shoes, and that is my loss."

Alex blushes.

Robert: "The succulent kid. *Capretto,* baby goat. Male. That is the matter of the Professor's conceit. The juicy kid in all his embodiments. For the tongue. Succulent."

Paternostra blushes.

Spina: "What do Albert's children have to do with this? You eat your kids, Albert?"

Cesso: "Sebastian, we don't eat our kids. That was the Greek way, as I'm told. We carry them fresh from the womb, straight into the garbage."

Spina: "Give us a break, Albert."

Cesso: "On the Parkway itself, as we all know except for Mr. Forza, our guest and newcomer. Mr. Forza, a case of attempting to flush a premature newborn down the toilet. The mother tried to force it down with the handle of the plunger, and then she flushed. After that she freshened up, because she felt that she had to go to the mall. But it wouldn't go all the way down. Somebody in the family had to use the toilet, and then that person flushed, and everything backed up. It came back up with the feces. Because not even a toilet can stomach this act."

Ayoub: "This is not a moral problem. This is a plumbing problem."

Cesso: "And this is what the police discovered in the toilet after she had to go to the mall because she was so upset, as she subsequently stated to the press. Dan Rather didn't mention it, they are so bored on the networks. The professor asked the question for Mr. Forza's benefit, since we all know that I have nine children, and now you know too, sir."

Robert: "The waste of the wasted child."

Alex: "So succulent. Uniquely marinated."

Spina: "For some reason, which I could never figure out, the word 'succulent' makes me nervous. It's not a word I appreciate in public."

Ayoub: "Because it causes you to contemplate the specialty of all of Utica's aldermen? The all-too-familiar act of sucking?"

Cesso: "Frankly, Louis, I don't understand your aggressivity this evening. You've been lashing out in all directions."

Raymond: "I'm not feeling comfortable here, Joseph. I'm going."

Paternostra: "Reconsider for my sake."

Raymond fixes himself another hotdog.

Paternostra: "Sebastian, I will say this only once, and I will say it very succinctly. When the subject of children arises, do not ever again make a snotty reference to Albert, who you well know in that category deserves only our admiration and for myself I would go so far as to say adulation is not too strong a word to use with reference to his gorgeous fatherhood. He doesn't founder, Mr. Forza. He's never foundered, for your information. No child of his, Professor Ayoub, will live as a foundling, like those animals who rule our streets in Cornhill, where we now all fear to drive through, even in the day time."

Spina: "I'm in complete agreement."

Raymond: "I'm totally aghast in this cellar tonight. We've been meeting here in harmony for how many years now? Until tonight, when we introduced a new element. We introduced dissension is what we introduced."

Spina: "I wouldn't go that far, Raymond. I wouldn't use the word 'element' in reference to our guests, and don't we all know why. I say, Okay, enough, let's get back to Utica. This is why whenever we gather together in Utica's name, my friends, we find ourselves in adhesion as a group. Frankly, Albert, in all honesty I respect your pro-life life style, but you have to admit that sometimes you bring it up when it has no place. You just can't wait to bring it up. I feel that you more or less raped this conversation

with your viewpoint, granted I, as a Catholic, agree with it, and
for that matter I agree with Joseph when he analyzes the black
problems of Cornhill and tells us that the father is absent from
that sector of town, missing in action, so to speak, who if he were
at home would be unleashing the terrorism that keeps those
families' noses clean."

Alex: "The depth of a father's love is defined by the level of
brutality which he's willing to lower himself into in order to do
the right thing, is the way I see it."

Raymond: "I never thought I'd agree with you."

Paternostra: "To the delightful Mr. Lucas, let us now raise a
glass."

They drink. Including Robert.

Ayoub to Alex: "You saved the night with your irony."

"Maybe the night, my infernal Professor, but you're beyond
salvation."

"I love this kid. I'm crazy about him."

"Hey! I'm no kid. I'm a big Billy Goat Gruff. Too tough and
smelly to eat."

Laughter all around. Then a vigorous attack on the meal, with
the exception of Robert, who nibbles. An outsider would remark
on the exceptional level of sound emitted, not related to conversation. The lip-smacking, the teeth-sucking, the numberless
indefinable mouth-noises that accompany the chewing, the swal-
lowing, the savoring. When they talk, they do not talk about
death and related Utica themes: The forty percent decline in the
city's population since the mid-fifties. The increasingly rare sightings
of persons (of all races) between the ages of twenty and forty. The
sooty air that they are forced to breathe. The calamitous departure of the textile mills. Followed by the departure of the three
General Electric plants. Then the closing of Griffiths Air Force
Base and the opening of The Marcy Detention Center for the
Criminally Insane. Followed by no more arrivals. These men have
grown weary of the incessant chatter of death. They talk about

the unbelievable weather. They talk about the current mayor, recently quoted in the *New York Times* as saying, "I'm the bum mayor of a bum town." Then settle on Spina's appearance on yesterday's late night news, and his claim that the fires and the street sign "desecrations" (Cesso's term, endorsed by all) were linked. Theories emerge: an undeclared anarchist movement; minority self-loathing; disgruntled firemen; slumlord arson; and, inevitably, someone among the numerous homeless insane who'd poured from the asylums when Washington and Albany became fiscally responsible. No consensus develops. Spina cannot defend his conspiracy theory. Robert speaks:

"Mr. Paternostra, the surname of your deep friend has yet to be uttered in my presence."

"Hudson. Raymond Hudson."

Cesso: "Raymond comes to us from the Coast. Like the late great movie star."

Spina: "Who turned out to be quite a queer, my friend."

Cesso: "Muzzy, must we now demean people for the gifts that God has given them? Have we descended into that pit? I don't think so."

Alex: "Homosexuality is a gift from God."

Ayoub: "Matter for a conceit."

Raymond, pedantically: "Rock Hudson hailed from the Midwest."

Paternostra, reverentially: "Rock Hudson was an enormous man."

Raymond: "In the spirit of hey! we're all getting along at last as a unit, I feel I should inform our guests that I acquire the little goats live from a farmer in Westmoreland because you can't get it in a store around here anymore. Not even in a butcher shop, because there aren't any more butcher shops in Utica. I acquire them on the night before and keep them in Joseph's backyard, where all night long they mow the lawn. See that big drain over there, Mr. Forza? One by one over there I open up their little throats into the drain. As I open up a given throat, the others are walking around, eating coal and cardboard. They walk around dropping raisins out of their cute little cans. I take off the heads, I rip out the guts, I skin. Then I wash down the area with pots of boiling water. This occurs about seven o'clock on the morning before grilling. Let's call that step one."

Robert: "And the Billy goat of lust, Professor Ayoub. Is your conceit sufficiently supple and relaxed to accommodate him as well?"

Ayoub: "The erotic goat of unreason."

Robert: "The goat of plunging Dionysian sex."

Ayoub: "With no concern for gender. With interest only in penetrative opportunity."

Robert: "Oral, ocular, anal, respiratory, and auditory. Perchance, perchance a vagina!"

Ayoub: "Eye holes, ear holes, nose holes. Holes, holes, holes and satyric penises of enormous proportions."

Robert: "Perchance to dream."

Raymond: "Anyone interested in step two? How about step two?"

Spina: "Will someone inform me as to why the intellectual people gravitate themselves constantly into the sewer? They go from where you can't understand them to where you don't want to."

Cesso: "Sebastian, we know that intellectuals love filth, but we don't know why."

Ayoub: "It buggers all understanding."

Paternostra, a sudden appearance of slight engorgement in the face, serenely: "What we know is they wallow."

Alex: "Quick, Raymond! Step two."

Raymond: "I insert my fingers. I rub the tender interior with lemon and garlic. Gently and thoroughly. Twenty minutes. I insert my fingers. I rub the interior with olive oil. Twenty minutes."

Cesso, proudly: "My youngest says, *The Three Baby Goats Guff,* tell me that story, Daddy."

Robert: "Professor Ayoub, the sternest of all challenges. How commodious is your conceit?"

"As commodious as Joseph's."

Raymond: "Joseph's what?"

Alex: "Tell us a story, Daddy."

Paternostra: "Is it not time for Mr. Forza to tell his story of our past?"

Cesso: "Yes. It is time, Mr. Forza."

Spina: "When have I ever disagreed with you, Albert? But now I think it's only fair to say that all of us would like a taste of what Joseph called your gorgeous fatherhood in high gear. Mr. Forza, will you defer yourself?"

Robert: "A consummation devoutly to be wished."

Raymond: "Come again?"

Robert: "Ah."

Paternostra: "I sense that you men need time to yourselves, in order to talk dirty in your own little ways. Am I wrong?"

Alex: "I believe that Mr. Forza has agreed to be our evening's concluding entertainment. Give us a taste, Mr. Cesso."

Cesso: "You all know it. *The Three Billy Goats Gruff.* There's no need to go on with this teasing."

Spina and Paternostra assure him that they've never heard it. Raymond and Alex claim they'd heard it as children but have forgotten. Ayoub asks Cesso if he will tell it in the sentimental-ized American adaptation, or in the spirit of the Norwegian original. Cesso replies that at home he has two editions corre-sponding to the alternatives and that his young ones much prefer the un-American version. Robert, who does not say whether or not he knows the tale, and is not asked, encourages Cesso to treat his adult audience as if it were composed of his young ones. He doesn't say "young ones." He says "your kids."

"Well, but I don't have the book. This will be rough. There are these three goats, once upon a time."

Ayoub: "Three Billys. All male."

"And they were of different ages. A very little one. A middle-sized one. And a big powerful one."

Ayoub: "The Terminator Billy."

"Oh yes, Louis. And he had two sets of horns. Four horns in all. Two spears and two round spirally things."

Ayoub: "In Norway, they call those spirally things the stones. Two spears and two stones."

"The idea of it is, that they've eaten all the grass on their side of the mountain, when they spy a wonderful lush mountainside that they can get to only by crossing a creaky old wooden bridge. So the little one goes first. Trip trap, trip trap."

Ayoub: "Was he urged on by the older two? Were they in their minds saying: Let the little shit pants go first. If he makes it safely, then we'll follow."

"This is not delved into, Louis. He's on the bridge, trip trap, trip trap, when suddenly from below a terrible troll says, I'm going to gobble you up. And the little Billy says, Don't gobble me up! I'm only a morsel. Why not wait for a solid meal? My bigger brother will come if you will only let me cross this scary bridge. So the troll goes for this plan and tells him he can cross over. And here comes the middle-sized goat."

Ayoub: "They saw that the shit pants made it. But just in case it wasn't safe, The Terminator sent the middle one on ahead. What choice did the middle one have?"

"Do you know what my youngest one said when she saw the illustration of the terrible troll? She said, Daddy, he's crying. I said, Why is he crying, Natalie? She said, Because he wants to see his mommy and daddy."

Ayoub: "Trolls are ugly supernatural dwarfs, who have no parents and prefer dank subterranean spaces."

Robert: "To wit: a cellar. Who among us here is a troll? Who among us here is not a troll?"

Paternostra: "Mr. Lucas is not a troll. He's a morsel!"

Robert finally smiles. The others cannot believe Paternostra's boldness and work to suppress the shock.

Raymond to Robert, brutally: "You definitely could play the role."

Robert to Raymond: "No, Mr. Hudson. I do not play. I *am* a troll. What say you to that, Professor Ayoub?"

Ayoub: "I say, Myself am hell."

Robert to Ayoub: "We understand each other, then, do we not?"

"Of course, the middle-sized Billy gets to cross over too, because he promises the troll a veritable feast."

Ayoub: "Do the shit pants and the teenager know how to trick the troll, or are they allegories of human ruthlessness? Let him eat the other guy, who cares if he's my brother, as long as he doesn't eat me."

Paternostra: "Consider, Professor, that they are brothers. This is a family. Consider the dimension of loyalty."

Ayoub: "Joseph, did you say 'loyalty'?"

"And so here comes the BIG BILLY GOAT GRUFF!!"

Ayoub: "In the Norwegian, it is said that his voice is as large, as ugly, and as hoarse as the troll's."

"And he, well, he simply destroys the troll. The illustration is quite graphic."

Ayoub: "The troll is dismembered, quartered, and pulverized by Big Billy Goat Gruff."

"And my kids just love that part! They just love it! The pulverization!"

Robert: "And so the three goats grew as fat as can be. And the sad troll found happiness at long last. Snip, snap, snout. This tale's told out."

Spina: "That's it, Albert?"

"That was the worst I ever told it."

Spina: "Oh, Albert."

"I'm sorry, Sebastian. I tell it better to my kids when we all sit together on the big comfy couch."

Paternostra: "You did very very well, Albert."

Cesso: "Mr. Forza, don't you think it's time?"

Spina: "Utica and the Founding Fathers. Alex promised us."

Robert: "Alex misheard. He should have told you Utica and its Founding Fathers."

Alex: "I didn't mishear."

Ayoub, beginning to warm to Robert, devil to devil: "Sebastian, you know that General George Washington came through the area before the founding of this country and this town, and you know why. We've discussed it too many times at our dinners. All the rich and the famous and the powerful and how they made their impact on our prehistory. We know this and we are bored. Mr. Forza will perhaps entertain us with stories of the obscure fathers. I believe that he wishes to surprise and delight us with new knowledge."

Paternostra: "What could possibly be new to you, Professor, I cannot imagine. I really cannot."

Ayoub: "Nor can I, Joseph. He will tell us what we cannot imagine, but that he can."

Raymond: "He'll make it up?"

Ayoub: "He'll weave the facts. He'll make a great tapestry with which we'll decorate this gloomy place."

Raymond: "He'll make it up."

Spina: "About our Utica, Professor, we don't make it up at these dinners."

Ayoub: "He'll weave the facts, Muzzy."

Robert: "Yes. I'll not invent the facts themselves."

Paternostra: "Mr. Forza, are your facts in a book where they may be checked?"

"Yes."

Paternostra: "Which book?"

"The book that I write as I speak it to you."

Ayoub, happily: "Springing from you as sin did spring from Satan's forehead?"

Robert: "Sin is real."

Cesso: "Sin is only the absence of good."

Robert: "The absence of good is real. The reality of this world is the absence of good. Would you agree, Mr. Paternostra?"

Paternostra: "I do not despair. Albert is good."

Ayoub: "Mr. Forza, you are a beautiful bird, and you have flown in through my window."

Robert: "Dramatis personae: William Cosby, colonial governor of New York, a scoundrel, a blackguard. Philip Schuyler, revolutionary hero. Rutger Bleecker, a wealthy man of Albany, a big-bottomed Dutchman, and a jolly shark. John Marchisi, Utica's original Italian, a virtuous fraud and a lover of children. *[Cesso beams.]* Alessandro Lucca, Utica's second Italian, Herculean Fool of Innocence. Primo Cesso, the elder, Utica's third Italian, Patriarch of all those who squatted here to rule. He ate the name of Lucca. He devoured it."

Because Robert pronounced "Cesso" in the proper Italian manner ("chesso"); because Spina, a third generation Italian-American, had virtually no Italian; because Paternostra, thanks to his gentle immigrant parents, had never heard the word; because Lucas and Hudson had no Italian; only Albert, whose relatives for decades had hidden their "Cesso" beneath the Americanized "Sesso," and Ayoub, who knew many things, were aware of the brutality, the direct assault of Robert's pronunciation. Like a seasoned teacher, Robert senses that he's spoken over the heads of his audience and must quickly take corrective measure: "Oh, how we Italians have borne the humiliation of our names! Consider this physique before you. Consider that, in my impoverished example, even to utter the word 'physique' is a mockery. And then consider how preposterous is Forza, how apparently ridiculous. How long, gentlemen, have your ears heard "Sesso" because in our shame we would not utter the vulgar term for toilet? To which American translations—the crapper, the john, even the shithouse—can do but scant justice. What's in a name? If not the body, then perhaps the soul? *Il cesso:* signifying the place of satisfying cessation, the terminal, where the digestive process bids its fond farewell to the body. Where things go down, and death is evacuated. *Il cesso:* a receptacle of death, yes? No. Please. Not a coffin. Please let us entertain no elegiac gestures of sentimental individualism. Not a personal *cesso,* but a public cemetery, a site of collective evacuations. The Greeks speak of the Bacchae. We must pay homage to the *Cessi.* Do I detect the faint odor of the sewage of your incredulity? How can you doubt me? The Land of Sun and Song has given us Perversi, Ribaldo, Crudo, Despoto, Lucifero, Falso, Pazzi, Cretinelli, Tizzone, Coardi, Cadavero, Mazzato, Caronia, Imbriaco, and Puzzoso: perverse, ribald, crude, despot, devil, false, crazy, little cretins, nigger, coward, corpse, murdered, carrion, drunk, and malodorous. Do you yet doubt me, gentlemen? When you return to your homes this evening, please, for my sake, consult your telephone directories for Culaperto: oh, yes, open anus. And Graziadei: the gift of God, a foundling. And Caccatovero: he who hath truly shat. Yes, *Paternostra.* Yes, *Spina.* And *Lentricchia.* Have you seen that one? A deliberate corruption of Lenticchia: yes yes, lentils, but a metaphor too in the beautiful vulgate of the peasant: Lenticchia, the scar left by the smallpox. I tell you, gentlemen, we Italians mean something."

Albert: reeling, wounded, silent.

Raymond: "How do you know that Rutger Bleecker had a big ass?"

Robert: "The detail doth intrigue you, Mr. Hudson?"

Spina and Paternostra: Leaning forward, loose jawed.

Ayoub, going for Albert's jugular, offers a toast: "*Andiamo al' cesso!*"

They all drink, even Albert, in his trance of pain fingering his crucifix.

Robert feels that he's growing, physically and vocally. Chalks up one silent victim. With one bold stare at Paternostra, says: "And when the Dutch sailed in, when those handsome sailors were afforded their first astonished glimpse of this paradise of the new world, as they floated in the bay of Manhattan, as they gazed with entranced attention, what was it that they saw but an ample and swelling bosom, which is how they wrote it down in their letters and in their journals, oh yes, always a bosom, from whose declivity was scattered in gay profusion the dogwood, the sumach, and the wild briar. It was an instance of a major, major experience that had flared periodically in the psyche from the beginnings of human time. And in the stupefied Dutch mentality, it was replayed once more, the originating instant of Greek mythology, the divinisation of the earth. The god of all gods, preceding all gods, was a goddess. She was Our Mother, whose womb swelled as the Virgin Mary's would, and from her came everything good, including Our Father, who was questionable. These good-looking Dutch sailors, gazing out upon the fresh, green breast of the new world, heard the heavy breathing and the dirty whisper. It was the whisper of the panderer, and they rushed to suck on it, they sucked on the pap of life and gulped down the incomparable milk of wonder. Our Mother? Our Whore? Did we, *do* we whore Our Mother? No matter. We would suck her dry."

Paternostra, rising, says, "Give me some air! Raymond, the trap door!" Then turning to Robert, and composing himself: "Mr. Forza. Next week, at the regularly scheduled dinner, I will hear you to your end." Spina and Cesso, a little confused, a little frightened, follow Paternostra and Raymond up the ladder, each saying: "Until next week."

Ayoub to Alex: "Your friend spoke the unspeakable, without quite speaking it. He may have gotten away with murder. His own. And then again. *[Turns to Robert.]* How is it that you, a newcomer, know Paternostra's nickname? Do you know the story behind it?"

"A curious footnote, Professor, buried deep in a famous book of the 1960s on the Mafia. And you too know the story behind the name, Professor, because the minor Lebanese stick-up artist who coined the unspeakable nickname and, it is said, suffered a punishment worse than death, was likely a friend of Grandfather Abraham Ayoub. Family secrets. Paternostra suspects that you know, but is too much of the old school to have a civilian slaughtered on the basis of suspicion. Not even the Mafia dares to murder a legendary Utica scholar. Professor Ayoub, Paternostra is a fool almost beyond our comprehension. He respects you, nay, he worships you, because he believes that you do not hunger for what he's gobbled up all of his life. He finds himself in awe, in the face of the more-than-human. You. The man of intellect. The man who has never been fondled by the desire for power. You. The godly man. This is Paternostra's tremendous illusion. And this you see. Paternostra's naiveté is the terrible goad of your epic self-loathing. And thus you speak so brusquely to him, with thinly veiled contempt. You wish to crush this vermin who reminds you of what you truly are. But what do you do in retaliation? You speak snottily. The man of intellect specializes in the subtly snotty retort. Quickly, now, Professor Ayoub, ascend the ladder before I lose control. Goodnight, Professor. *Ci vediamo.*"

Without a word, Ayoub leaves.

Alex, petulantly: "Almost nothing about Utica's founders. Nothing whatsoever about the fires and the street signs. What do we get? Toilets and tits. The least you could do is give me the story on Paternostra."

"I find extended exposure to humans so exhausting."

John, at trap door: "Hurry up, please, it's time."

"Tell me how he got his unspeakable nickname, which you spoke but didn't speak. Then you can go to sleep."

"It was sometime in the middle fifties. More or less, I believe, about the time I left this city. Paternostra decided to drop in on a certain high-stakes crap game. He was, of course, the producing agent. In the previous month, this game had been held up twice. Paternostra decided to drop in. In order to issue a warning should the brazen robber decide to make another appearance. Give back the money and all will be forgotten. We don't do these things to each other. Etcetera. The robber made an appearance, waving his big pistol. Paternostra made a brief and civilized statement. The robber is said to have responded, 'You think I'm afraid of you?' He put the pistol to Paternostra's temple. Then he told Paternostra to strip himself naked. Paternostra did so. And this was the first shock to most of the men there, though not to Paternostra's closest associates, and not, apparently, to the robber himself. The sight of Paternostra's chest was a hammer on the skull. He was a man of about fifty. No tone in the pectorals. None. Perhaps it was some hormonal imbalance. Who can say? There they were, for all intents and purposes, female breasts. Yes, purposes. The robber said, 'Now you all know why Mr. Big Shot is called "Our Mother" behind his back.' Alex, this was a very bad moment. The people there wanted to evaporate. They wanted to become un-born, because they felt that they would not be forgiven for hav-ing seen what they saw. A week or so later, four of them actually moved out of state as a precaution. So it is said. But there is more, Alex. The second shock. The robber issued an instruction to Paternostra's body guard, a brutal killer himself, a ladies' man, by the way. The robber said, 'Rosario, you want your boss's brains on the ceiling? Suck his tits now.' Rosario hesitated. 'Suck his tits or I'll kill you both.' This robber had quite a reputation for extreme hot headedness. Rosario did what he was told. Alex, this was such a bad moment in that room, I can't begin to phrase it. But there was a third shock in store for all. A hitherto unknown event in the history of sexuality. We're talking about the 1950s, Mr. Wise Guy. Mr. Know It All. As Rosario sucked his nipple, Paternostra's member achieved sterling tumescence. Alex, Paternostra ejaculated. Then the robber made Paternostra put the money into a sack. Snip, snap, snout. This tale's told out."

"This is a true story?"

"Yes."

"It's in a book?"

"Tastefully hinted at in a footnote."

"The tit of the new world. Paternostra's tits. Rosario. The sailors who greedily sucked."

"As I told it, I restrained myself from trying to determine what, if anything, stirred in that ninety-year-old crotch."

"I applaud your self-control. But who will be the innocent bystander who gets killed when they come for you?"

"Melodrama, my dear Alex. Mere melodrama."

"What was the fate suffered by the Lebanese stick-up artist, worse than death?"

"I don't know."

Big John, growling: "I said it's time."

"The footnote cited a rumor."

"What was it?"

"Something involving a child."

"Any specifics in the rumor?"

"I don't remember."

"I don't believe you."

Over the trap door, Big John looms.

Chapter 7

As they walk into the realty office Alex spots the light flashing on his answering machine: "This is Alderman Spina calling at approximately 10:47 P.M. on the Fourth. According to Joseph, we have a change in group plans. Tomorrow night, same time, same place. Joseph says every night in the cellar at eight from now on, because once a true story starts, you can't put it down until it's all over, whether you like it or not. According to Joseph, be there. My personal message to my new friend, Mr. Forza, is Hello to you, Mr. Forza, feel free to visit your new home of the near future any time you like. Mr. Lucas, to you I say let's wrap up the paper work as soon as you can, because this transition period amounts to nothing more than a tremendous pain in my ass, and I'm ready to move out any time this guy wants to move in as soon as possible. Until tomorrow, this is Sebastian Spina signing off, in case you didn't recognize the voice known to the vast majority of my fellow citizens. God bless."

"Looks like you made a big hit, even with Joseph."

"I'm prepared."

"To be hit?"

"Yes. That too."

"I'm going to call Heather."

"Good."

"Right now."

"The urgency of passion!"

"Robert."

"The pain!"

"Robert."

"It would give me the greatest pleasure to audit the master."

"Hey!"

"Yes?"

"Go to your room."

"Tell me just one fact, then I'll comply."

"No."

"Please. The glorious Heather's surname."

"Faxton."

"Faxton?"

"Faxton."

"Faxton!?"

"You deaf or what?"

"Ah, Faxton."

"What do you mean by 'ah'? What's that supposed to mean?"

"*Buona sera,* my good Alex."

————————⟫•0•⟪————————

The next morning, after breakfast, Alex makes a call to Spina and then informs Robert that everything is moving ahead rapidly and he'll need to make a major deposit at a savings and loan. Without a word, Robert goes to his room and returns with the bank check. Tells Alex to deposit it in his, Alex's account, because he, Robert, has no intention of ever going into a bank again.

"You're saying deposit a thing of this magnitude in my own name?"

"Seventy for Spina, forty-two hundred for yourself, and the rest to me, to be apportioned by you, penuriously, with maximum penuriousness! on a monthly basis, until I die. What remains after death is yours."

"I can't accept the forty-two hundred."

"Why?"

"Since I'm the only agent involved, I can only accept three percent, which amounts to twenty-one hundred clams is all I've got coming to me."

"Please do exactly as I say. You have a great deal coming to you."

"You're trying to buy a caretaker."

"I want care. Yes."

Alex falls silent.

"Really, Alex, what is there for you to do? Wherein lies the inconvenience? A thin envelope of cash, no checks please, once a month. [Pause.] In person, of course."

"I'll mail it."

"We'll see each other, once a month, and this will be quite rewarding, even for you. You bring me enough to meet my meager needs and we enjoy a little conversation, about your increasingly complex life with the visionary Heather, who pulls you from the grave even as we speak. You, Alex, are Eurydice, and she is your Orpheus. And I, Alex, I too am Eurydice, and you will play the part of my Orpheus."

"That story turns out pretty lousy."

"Together, we triumph."

"Lousy for all concerned."

"Together we suffer collective redemption."

"Then what?"

"Original dialogue ensues."

Long silence.

"When do you see Heather?"

"This afternoon."

"Where?"

"Why?"

"Tell me where."

"So you can accidentally drop in?"

"I won't drop in, I promise. Although I would love to."

"Café Caruso."

"Alas, I've a prior engagement. A walk in the harsh glare of day to see an old black man. In lieu of on-site counseling, at the café itself, I give you one guideline for the thrilling meeting you are about to have. You can never get too far ahead of yourself. Never can you proceed too quickly in affairs of the heart. Heather will need to know all about the current Caroline Lucas, in whose development she will undoubtedly take a strong hand."

"You enjoy this, don't you?"

"The demonstrative pronoun reference is vague."

"Planning my life."

"Unquestionably."

"Robert, I'm in the dark. You owe the caretaker a few of your main facts. Or no deal."

"I'll tell you everything. Everything. For forty-two years, after I left Utica, I lived in a cellar. In Manhattan. In the bookstore where I worked. I lived without intimacy, as a troll. I was looking for my mommy and daddy. Now you know my main facts. Have we a deal, Alex?"

Silence.

"Give me a minute to grasp the rich array of your biographical data."

"A deal?"

"You won't feed off my life. Never."

"Alex."

"That's not going to happen."

"Robert Tagliaferro is a troll, not a sucking parasite. We don't confuse you with our mommy and daddy."

"Obviously. I'm too young."

"Nor is your daughter, who is younger yet, and quite helpless, a sucking parasite, which is not obvious to you."

"Spare me the lecture."

"Why?"

At last, the freakish cold spell, which all Uticans insist is only average summer weather, has broken. In sunglasses, without the watch cap, in a white T-shirt and Caroline's blue jeans, Robert heads out north again on Pellettieri Ave, this time not all the way to lifeless Broad, but turning right on Catherine, for the six-block walk east, to the three-story, six-family tenement of his youth. He doesn't walk: he strolls, stopping frequently, looking up eyes shut into the sun, counting to twenty. Sun glare off a white bald dome. All those years in the steep canyons of Manhattan, years of the cellar, had robbed him of natural color, had actually lightened him, and now he'd get some color back. Catherine on the way out, and Bleecker, he decided, at last, on the way back.

The changes in ethnic presences would hold no surprises for him, but he had not prepared for, could not have prepared for, this terrible quiet, late morning on a perfect summer day. These long vistas of silence. The open lots on Broad were another thing. They'd been a fixture even in the fifties. But Catherine had always been a street crowded with two-family houses, spitting-distance separated. An exuberant, dirty street of hard Italian-American life. Now, on Catherine, houses burned, abandoned, vandalized. In between the standing structures, a few perfectly maintained with fresh paint and wrought iron, there they are: lots of trash and unruly vegetation. And lots paved (for what purpose?), chain-link fenced, empty. And lots of well-kept lawns.

Kept by whom? Why? Also enclosed with chain-link fencing. More than the dirt piles, the broken furniture, the broken tricycles in front yards; the rusted hulks of automobiles, the boarded-up windows: it's the openness of Catherine. Actual "views" now where there had been only claustrophobic containment. The well-kept empty lots more chilling than the trashy ones. The houses showing pride of ownership sadder than the wrecked shacks.

⇒►◦◄⇐

Morris opens the door and without the slightest of pauses says, "You forgot to bring your envelope," then stands there staring at Robert, who replies, "Can I come in?" Morris says, "Why? Why should I let you in?" Turns and walks back into the room, to a bare wood rocker beside a window giving a view of the perfect bricks of St. Anthony of Padua. Robert enters, shuts the door, and with a clarity he could not have managed two nights before, takes in the old man and the room. The same carpet, worn down now in the traffic patterns to the floor boards. Everything else unfamiliar. A room full of unfinished furniture: raw, lean, and clean, like the old man himself, this old man full of the cool fury of contempt: "You come here crowding in on the lunch hour, but don't expect me to feed you," and Robert responding, "I didn't come here to eat," and the old man quickly back at him: "Because why should I feed you? Who said I have to?" And Robert: "I came again to talk." And the old man: "While I eat? You want to crowd me with talk and watch me eat?" Then Robert with his old stand-by: "Wherein lies the harm?" The old man: "You ever try to sit in your own home and let a stranger watch you eat? A person who is allowed to watch you eat in your own home has to be an intimate person, a friend, or a wife, or a beloved child. You don't qualify. Pretty soon I'm going to start in on the pork n' beans. I'll give you the top part of the can I take off with the can opener. You can join me for lunch and eat the vicious lid. Then I'm going to eat the banana pudding I made for dessert, enough for an army and none for you. If you watch me eat, I'll get stomach tension, there's the harm, and I don't want it, but I don't want to feed you either. So I guess I better not eat, you son of a bitch." After this monotoned tirade, Robert says something softly that involves the use of the word "relent," which causes Morris to use the words "coward" and "baby" on the way to an unanswerable conclusion: "You didn't stop for forty-two years and now you want me to quit after two days? What are you worth? Anything?"

Robert takes a chair from the dining table and carries it to within a couple of feet of the rocker, which is angled at the side of the window, so that the sitter can with a small turn of the head take in the view. Robert positions his chair directly in front of the window, so that he can take in Morris and St. Anthony's at the same time. He says, tapping his head, "I have the contents of the envelope in here." Morris replies, "I'm not taking the bait." Robert says, "The Taliaferros of America, without the letter 'g.' They have banished the letter 'g,' the Italian connection has been buried in a shallow grave. All of it is here," tapping his head, and then Morris, leaning over, tapping Robert's head, replies: "You mean in your ass?" Robert laughs hard, evoking a flicker of a smile from Morris. Then Robert, still grinning: "I want the facts that you denied me in my childhood."

"If I do, then maybe you can get out of here for good. Then I can eat the pork n' beans in peace. Okay. We got you from a light-skinned black family in a town in the northeast corner of Pennsylvania. But you were not born there and they were not your parents, unless maybe they lied to us. This black family was related to one of Melvina's friends who knew what we wanted and couldn't have. We were poor and you were free. Where you were born, or who your blood parents were, we never asked, because we didn't care. Why should we have cared? And didn't want you to care either, we were such fools, because you cared anyway, and look at you now. May God have mercy on you.

They wrote down your name because they said that the people that they got you from said someday it'll make him happy and proud to have such a name, because Booker T. Washington had that name too, that's what the 'T' stands for in Booker T. But without the 'g.' They said you were named 'Robert' because 'Robert' meant bright with fame. How wrong they were. 'Robert' in my understanding means corroded with ingratitude. Okay. Now you can get out of here for good."

"Samuel T. Rayburn too."

"That a fact? Rayburn I believe was involved in the killing of President Kennedy. Which is a thing that Booker T. wouldn't have done. Booker was black."

"And Clay Taliaferro, a famous dancer I saw perform once in New York. A very tall man with the map of Italy all over his face. A charismatic black. He danced a black general who married a white woman from Venice."

"There you go. Problem in a nutshell."

"He killed her."

"Naturally. *[Pause.]* There was a pretty good middleweight fighter from around here when you were little, with the 'g' in, just like you. He was an Italian and the Italian people in this neighborhood said prayers for him, but it didn't help. Which one of these is your kin? Rayburn?"

"The name of Aunt Melvina's friend who made the contact?"

"Dead."

"The name of that town in Pennsylvania?"

"Melvina told me long ago that they moved."

"Where to?"

"Can't remember."

"Their name, at least, you must remember."

"Can't remember. Ask Melvina."

"Were the people who handed me over to the people in Pennsylvania Italian or black or both?"

Morris looks at the church.

"I see. And this is the form of your revenge. To withhold knowledge from a man whose life's blood is knowledge."

Morris looks at the church.

"You intend to torment me."

"That Italian restaurant I used to take you to kitty-corner from the church. I took you there for Italian chitlins, which those people call tripe. I loved tripe. Nothing like it. Truth is, I like it better than chitlins. Those damn Italians. That restaurant changed hands not too long ago."

"The Modernistic. Whenever we went, they brought me extra little dishes of Italian good things."

"You can't get tripe there any more. Son of a bitch. I went in once for it. They said, Oh my God, that's a thing of the past. The old-timers, they said. They turned red when I said the word 'tripe' in there. Oh yeah. I said, you know, I'm an old-timer. I told them my grandmother came over from the southern side of Sicily, where they had a considerable amount of warm interaction with the people of Africa. You know what the waiter said? We don't like political discussions in here of an irritating variety. Take your business elsewhere."

"Were the people who handed me over to the people who handed me over to—"

"Maybe the original people who started all the handing over weren't the original people who started it."

"Nevertheless, were the—"

"Consult the dead. That's your specialty, isn't it?"

"Your answer is an evasion."

"The new owners of the Modernistic gave it a new name. They call it The New Modernistic."

"You won't help."

"You smell moldy. You're dead, Robert, like The New Modernistic."

"Give me just a little help, Uncle Morris."

"I recommend you have your lunch over there."

Robert stares out the window. Morris stares at Robert. Morris covers his face with his hands. Seems like forever. Removes hands. Speaks: "All the churches still look good in this neighborhood." Robert replies, "I saw Mt. Carmel on the way over."

"Like a pretty picture."

"The churches don't belong here anymore."

"Robert, it's starting to leave my system. I want it to stay, but it's leaving."

"What?"

"My anger."

Silence.

"Robert, I need to forgive you, but I hope I'll never love you again. What's in that envelope in your mind, because I don't want to talk about us. Talk to me about those white and black Taliaferros without the 'g.' And those Italians who don't want to associate with the white or black Taliaferros, so they put in a 'g.'"

"The 'g' was there from the beginning, and the beginning was an Italian invention. Tagliaferro. *Il tagliaferro*. The iron cutter. It is unknown and unknowable, when the beginning was. Or who it was who said, 'I am the beginning. I, Who Am Who Am, name myself Tagliaferro. For I am *il tagliaferro,* am I not? Now let there forever be Tagliaferros, and let them go forth from this place, bearing my mark and memory.' Like Eden, the site of origination is itself unknown. What we know are the places they scattered themselves to, as they trudged, sailed, and rode across the surface of the earth: France, England, Scotland, the American colony of Virginia, and then the states: North Carolina, Alabama, Florida, Texas, Michigan, Wyoming—yes! Wyoming! And what do we call this scattering, this diffusion, this differentiation from intimacy, of a single people from a single and bounded place on the earth? This splintering into different spellings and different colors of the same? We call it being thrown into the world."

"Say what?"

"We call it how it is in the world. Our thrown-ness. Our ejectedness."

"The place for people who talk like you is well known. They call it The Marcy Detention Center for the Criminally Insane."

"The people who handed me over to the people in that little town in the northeast corner of Pennsylvania—"

"Who said it was a little town? I said town, just town."

"The people who first handed me over—"

"Stop it! I told you we can't be sure who started the handing over. We just know you were handed. Same as your story about those Taliaferros, we can't say about the beginning. I don't know where any of them came from. I don't know whether they were black or white or even goddamn Italian. Nobody said you were their daughter's illegitimate child, either, which is a guess you haven't made yet, but which you could. For all I know, Melvina's friend in Utica who made the contact, well, maybe she was the one, she was the mother maybe, and felt sorry for Melvina and brought you to that town straight west from here and then made up that whole story so that we could have you free of charge and free of the pressure from the person whose womb you fell out of. Maybe."

"Was Aunt Melvina's friend white or black?"

"Guess."

"Certainly black! She could not, at that time, and in this place, have had an intimate white friend. Not possible in a northern state."

"Maybe Melvina's friend ran with white men. How about that?"

"In the absence of facts, what are we talking about? Give me more facts."

"Tell me more about those people with or without the 'g.' Talk funny some more."

"The first Taliaferro came to America from England, where the 'g' was banished. Once, in England, far back, there were many

Taliaferros, but most converted themselves into Toliver, because they felt exposed. They feared a name that would be traced outside the Anglo-Saxon gene pool. And now there are Tolivers in deep disguise in this country who favor names like Harold and Henrietta. And they have scattered to California, Oregon, and Washington state. But the first American Taliaferro was intrepid. A man amazed by his Italian heritage, who would go no farther than to drop 'g' as a concession to the phonetic laws of England. A man with political friends in the mother country, who came to the colonies in 1645, where he was granted thousands of choice acres free in Virginia. A plantation gentlemen. An owner of many slaves."

"Free land. Integrated rape."

"Perhaps even integrated love, Uncle Morris. Booker T had to give himself the name of Washington."

"Because Booker T was sly."

"His mother was a slave who was maybe proud to give her son the name Taliaferro. Because maybe she loved the father, who loved her. Think of that, Uncle Morris."

"You think of this: She was maybe proud of that name because she loved the father, but Booker didn't love the father, so he figured it out that if he had to have the name of a white father he might as well implicate the white father of our country. Because Booker was comical. You yourself ought to be more like Booker. Try to be comical as long as you're going to be sitting here all this time and crowding my lunch time and giving me tension. Why don't you give me a little relief, Robert?"

"The first Taliaferro in America was called Robert."

"I hate coincidences. They always spoil the story."

"Robert Taliaferro. You will find him in a book."

"Who decided he was tired of the splinterings and the diffusions all over the face of the earth. Who decided he wanted to get back to the oneness at the beginning, in the first place. So what did he do? He fucked a black woman, because this is the preferred highway back to Eden, which they said was the Middle East, but they were wrong. It was somewhere in Italy, before they became ashamed of tripe. I can talk crazy too, Robert. Anybody can do it with the least imagination."

"Robert Taliaferro is a fact of history. Do not scorn him. The westward journey of Tagliaferros from Italy into France in the eleventh century is a fact. In the old French they became Taillefer. They wanted to be French. Because they wanted no memories. We are happily bereft of ancestry! Their emergence in England is a fact, after the Battle of Hastings. Across the Atlantic they sailed, always west in search of virgin land: New thresholds! New names! New identities! *I tagliaferri*: those who cut irons, the shackles of history. These are truths. I have consulted many venerable volumes. Yes, they impregnated black slaves. Their own, to whom they tied the shackle of a name. Henry, Thomas, James, Sinclair, William, Hardin: in Florida, Michigan, and so on. Wyoming! All of them with ancestors in Virginia. The women are not named. Obviously, the black mothers are not mentioned. Lawyers, judges, mathematicians, professors of microbiology and English, presidents of banks, directors of cemeteries, a confederate general, and a Baptist minister in North Carolina who wrote comic sketches."

Morris roars: "At last my relief."

"William Taliaferro. Take this seriously. Please. Born in Virginia in 1895. Listen to me, Uncle Morris. A research scientist at the University of Chicago. All the books say that he died without issue in 1973. His dates fascinate me. Earlier generations of Taliaferros could not have known Italian immigrants. William the scientist is another matter. A young man in Chicago, working too hard in his laboratory. Cooped-up constantly in the airless room of his rotted thought. He finds, but how? an Italian woman of shocking vitality, married to a loutish bricklayer. He lurches. He abandons the death watch over his own corpse. He lunges lifeward."

"Your daddy was a white bookworm with some black blood mixed up in him, who lived in a chicken coop. Your mama was a shocking Italian peasant, who electrocuted the Chicago professor. I'm hungry now. I'm starving. This Robert Taliaferro, this Robert the first, fathered the maternal grandfather of George Washington, who (the maternal grandfather, not George) illicitly fathered the child who fathered the child who was Booker's father. In other words, this Taliaferro is the secret link between the blacks and the whites, and maybe even the Italians, and you have returned from the dead to be the Great Multicultural Hope. I'm going to eat now whether you watch or not. In his spare time, Taliaferro the Shackler originated the Sons of Italy. Your name means the iron cutter, is that a fact?"

"Yes."

"Well, then, least you could do is become a crap cutter. Cut the crap, Robert."

Then Morris rises, says follow me, and they head to the kitchen, where Morris opens two cans of pork n' beans, heats the contents, sets the table for two, all the while saying not a word as Robert sits defeated and dejected, with so many more Taliaferro details to pass on but no more heart for the task. Morris says, "I'm serving you some because I intend to eat my lunch in peace. That's the only reason. Do the dead eat actual food or do they just feed on the living?"

"In one of the books I found a picture of him."

"The cooped-up professor?"

"He must have been about your age at the time."

"Any resemblance to you?"

"Perhaps."

"Just so many faces to go around."

Silence.

"I'm not unhappy to be here."

"Say what?"

"I fear to declare it positively."

"Cut the crap. You want any bread?"

Morris ladles out the pork n' beans. Pours two glasses of ice water. Eats with gusto. Robert attempts a spoonful. Drinks. Robert says, "He bears some resemblance to you, too."

"William is probably your uncle."

"Who's my father?"

"Me. And you are my long lost, my shackled son. Welcome home, son."

━━━━➤•0•◄━━━━

He had thought that on the way back he might break his word to Alex and sneak a peek into Café Caruso, but when he leaves Morris he knows that he doesn't have the strength of body or heart to confront Bleecker. He returns the way he came, slower of step in midday heat, drained, head oddly warm, straight to bed. When he awakes in late afternoon, he's feverish and queasy and the top of his head, the white bald dome, is on fire: scorched by sustained exposure to unfamiliar sun. The realty office is empty, and when he knocks on Alex's door he gets no response. Too tired to descend, he sits on the floor before the door, huddled into himself, shivering. Many minutes later, almost six o'clock, two hours to go before the second dinner at Joe's, Alex is home, up the stairs he comes, feeling none too lively himself. When he sees Robert struggling to his feet he says, "You look the way I feel." Robert manages: "Your meeting with Heather Faxton was a fiasco?" Alex replies, "No. Just me. I was the fiasco."

Nurse Alex attends to Robert: with two aspirin for the small fever, with chicken broth (from a can) for the queasiness, with an ointment, vividly green, plastered all over the burning dome. Within an hour, the feverish effects of sun-blast have worn off, the stomach is settled, the dome is soothed. Alex says, "By eight, you'll be ready to rock, but the ointment stays on for twenty-four hours according to what it says on the tube." Robert requests a report on "the fiasco of Café Caruso."

"Not a lot to say. I was nervous."

"Tell me more."

"I was self-conscious. Stupid."

"More."

"I could tell you she liked me."

"But this I already told you."

"She was relaxed. She's older than me. Early thirties is my guess."

"In your nervous condition you communicated that you liked her. You communicated shyness. You fear, of course, that you communicated weakness. You did not. You communicated decency. And, we suspect, too much self-reserve. Your withholdment was also communicated."

"She communicated strength."

"At Caruso's you were not overwhelmed with erotic thoughts. This is what you call your weakness."

"No comment."

"The poet Marvell has already commented on your fate and Heather's together. You will roll all your strength and all your sweetness up into one ball and tear your pleasures with rough strife—through the iron gates of life."

"She is not coy, Robert."

"Neither are you."

Alex manages a smile but no words.

"Your fate and Heather's is to share a long and happy life."

"Are you ready for tonight?"

"Give in, Alex."

"If I don't?"

"Death—absolute and without memorial."

Chapter 8

He begins, "Dear Heather," then crumples the sheet of paper, heart racing, and tosses it (the paper, wishing it could be the heart) into the basket beside his realty office desk. Stares down at legal pad. How could such a letter be written without protective cover? He, write "dear?" The phone. Let it ring. The answering machine, the voice of Heather Faxton saying, "Come to dinner soon whenever you're free. I had fun this afternoon." Protective cover, sent by God. He would respond with maximum restraint.

———◆———

7:02 P.M.
July 5

Heather,

    I'll be happy to come to dinner soon whenever I'm free. I'm always free, so just pick out any night and let me know and I'll be happy to come right over. I had fun too, whether it showed or not.

I've just read what I wrote and see that I've let something out of the bag right off the bat, which is how Robert would want it. Without saying a word concerning the major subject between us I think that we made it clear to each other this afternoon that something is going on. If I'm wrong about this on your behalf, what an ass I've just made of myself. What an ass! I'm delivering this personally sometime later tonight, so I'll know by tomorrow if I have completely humiliated myself. My guess is that Robert would say that I did the proper thing in any event. We'll see. He'd probably also say something like I took a step up on my own to climb out of the coffin I've lived in since the day my wife died a little over two years ago. You already knew about my wife. You already knew about my daughter living in New York with my sister-in-law who couldn't be a better person. Like Robert, you know a lot. You didn't flinch. I flinched. But I didn't totally flinch because after all I am writing this, and I'm definitely bringing it to your house. I flinched because why don't I just call you instead of writing this? I have some courage but maybe at the present time not enough. I never thought that I'd know a woman like you with your I don't know the word for it. All I can think of is the word reality. When I'm in the same room with you I sense all of you in the room and not even a particle of your mind is someplace else. This is powerful. This is unnerving. Here's a question for you. If you're reality, what am I? Robert says that although I am dead, I can come back if I want to. My wife used to say everything is possible. We'll see. Maybe I am unreality.

Since about three days ago when I ran into Robert and decided against my will to take him in, I feel that I've entered a whirlpool. I ran into that sportscaster Nick LeoGrande and all of a sudden I'm telling him that I'm quitting competitive golf. Out of the blue I said this to

LeoGrande, I never planned it, and even while I'm saying it, even before I finish saying it, I'm feeling terrific all of a sudden because suddenly I realize how much I hate to be involved in competition. I *hate* competition. I can't give people a line when I show them a house. *They* have to live there, not me, so what use is my opinion? I can't stomach business people or politicians because they feed off of living flesh, all of them without exception do this except you, who charge much too little for your various rentals even in this depressed market in this city where they invented depression. I have to make a living so my hands are dirty too to a certain extent. I have a business. Nobody is forcing me to make a living through business, granted, but the freedom you get in the real estate game in this ghost town is phenomenal. Only a college professor gets more.

Robert arrives and I take into my home a complete stranger who is maybe insane. I give up competitive golf on the 11 o'clock news (which you never mentioned, which nobody has yet mentioned). I am writing this letter to you, with everything it contains, which proves that I am also insane. Robert is giving me more money than I earned, much more, and he's more or less given me an inheritance. If you saw the size of the check he asked me to deposit in my own name, if you saw how little this guy requires, then you would understand what I'm inheriting from a total stranger. Why me? Because I took him in? It is not like me to have taken him in, or anybody, in. Because I arranged for him to go to these dinners? Because he knows all the stories? I think he knows something about my family history that I don't know about and about everybody else who has ever lived in this town for the last two hundred years. My favorite professor at Utica College once said in class whoever knows the stories has all the power because we're anxious to give ourselves away to the storyteller, or something like that. I think his actual words might have been "We seek to be enthralled." I admit that's an idea I like. Just a few minutes ago I said to Robert that I had the feeling that he somehow knew all about the weekly dinners at Joe's, who the diners were and so forth, because I sensed that he was prepared to "go on" like a man who does a one-man show. His exact answer to me was, "The laws of probability would probably not exclude our prior knowledge." He knows who you are, Heather. I think he knows your family history, God forbid. I'm positive from a hint he gave me this morning. It never occurred to me to link Faxton with the name of the hospital (where my wife died, by the way). You arrived almost two years ago, is that right? The normal question is why would a woman of your unusual qualities leave San Francisco and come to Utica? Just to restore a beautiful old apartment building on Genesee Street and then charge a ridiculous rent that ensures you're losing money? My guess is that your ancestors lived in this town. Heather, forgive me for saying this, but in some ways you remind me exactly of Robert himself. You two are the whirlpool I have entered— or is it the whirlwind? Is there a difference? Either way, I feel that I'm being taken in and eventually taken over. Is this what you get when you quit competition? What is your thought on that topic?

In closing, I have two thoughts. Number one: I am told that no woman has ever attended the dinners in Joe's cellar, which have been going on for years. Wouldn't it be amazing if you were the first? If I asked Paternostra, I think it would happen since he seems partial to me. Number two: The view from your house is no doubt like the view of the city I enjoy on some of the back nine holes at Valley View. The beauty of this view of the city is that you look down on the city and you can't see it. You see a valley. You see a sea of green. You see a stillness. The tops of trees and a couple of church spires. Not even the gold dome bank from your road.

From such a point of view you don't think of the green sea as a canopy, which is what it is. You don't think about what's under the canopy, because there's always something under a canopy. You look and you're almost happy and would be totally happy if only the church spires disappeared.

Sincerely yours,

Alex

————————————————

Alex looks up from the legal pad and out to Joe's. Paternostra, Raymond, Ayoub, Cesso, and Spina arrive at the same moment. They glance at the realty office. They huddle. No gestures, no bobbing of heads. The huddle tightens. Then they go in. From behind him, Robert has entered. Alex hears Robert say: "They believe that they can prepare themselves for me."

The Second Dinner

The room of drinkers and cardplayers goes silent. Where's John? They're at the trap door when a voice sings out: "It's okay, John." They descend, catching the receding voices of this exchange:

"What's that green garbage on his head?"

"You don't know?"

"What?"

"Blood."

Down into the cellar of agitated voices, quickly quelled by their appearance.

Ambassador Spina stands, bows: "How fortunate to see you again, precisely when your votes are required to break this deadlock among friends. The roll has been called. Joseph abstains. Raymond is for death. Personally, I support death. Albert, our Prime Minister of Pro-life, stuns us all. He's in favor of immediate release and the dropping of all charges. Professor Louis votes reluctantly with Albert. Professor Louis complains that Albert doesn't go 'nearly far enough,' whatever that means, let God spare us the explanation of one of his lectures, unless he knocks it off in twenty-five words or less, what do you say, Professor?"

Raymond, a right-hander, is sliding his right hand under his apron.

Alex, eyeing Raymond, is aghast. Robert is cool: "Good, Raymond. Absent me from misery."

Raymond's hand finds it: to scratch, to rearrange. Recalled to consciousness, out of touch, Raymond says, "You talking to me, Little Green Troll?"

"This is what I say," says the Professor. "A parent's rights take precedence. How many words is that, Muzzy?"

Paternostra, beaming: "The professor suggests that public apologies are in order?"

"From the media, from the police, from the courts."

"Yes," says Paternostra, "from the police."

"Hey!" says Alex the impetuous. "What's the subject here?"

"The Parkway baby killer," says Spina. "Today we were finally recognized on CNN. How do you two vote?"

Cesso takes the floor: "Preliminary forensic findings indicate that the baby was breathing before it was forced down the toilet to drown. Blunt force trauma is indicated via the plunger handle and is said to be possibly co-fatal. These are what they call the facts of the case."

Robert, nose in the air: "And Mr. Hudson has once again denied me kid. Mr. Hudson, you have created perhaps pizza in the proper manner, from scratch, have you not?"

"Don't use that word pizza."

Spina: "What are you doing under that apron, Raymond? Is that a pistol you got under there, or are you just happy to see Mr. Forza? Heh! Heh!"

"How's your sore throat? This thing will lubricate your throat, Muzzy."

Spina guffaws again as Robert, with longing, says, "Mr. Hudson, I crave your what shall I call it?" and Paternostra says, "Boys, reduce the filth," and Alex, who's heard enough, says, "I vote for the nuthouse. You want my vote? Send her to Marcy where she belongs. Remove the ovaries as a gesture to the unborn."

Spina: "And you, Mr. Forza?"

Raymond: "Stab her up the ovaries."

Paternostra: "I am disgusted."

Spina: "Mr. Forza?"

"I vote for elaborately extended discussion of this grievous topic and all issues bearing upon it, however fantastically. I've come to tell you stories, and to eat, not vote. Mr. Hudson, when? *[Sniffs.]* The aromas of your art stagger me."

Cesso: "She is in custody."

Robert: "Who?"

Cesso: "She is arraigned. She is charged preliminarily with child endangerment and disturbing the peace. She awaits trial."

Robert: "Who? Tell me her name."

Cesso: "For an act that doctors commit with impunity even late in the third trimester."

Spina: "Forgive us, Father Cesso, for we have sinned."

Cesso: "They crush the skull. They suck out the brains when the head is two inches from the light of this world."

Alex: "The what of this world?"

Raymond: "But they don't order a pizza from Domino's one hour later. They don't go to the mall."

Cesso: "Even doctors eat. Sometimes twenty minutes later. They go home. With their kids they watch Sesame Street. They vacuum rugs. They make love after they have done this deed of the clinics. On the same day, they call their mothers in Florida and say the usual stupid things about the weather. I love you, Mom."

Spina: "Is the fucking world supposed to stop, Albert?"

Raymond: "This bitch probably said, Kid, eat shit and die."

Cesso: "Yes, the world is supposed to stop. No, Raymond, she is not full of hate. Her demeanor at the mall was described as kind and placid by the clerk in the CD Super Store. The Domino's delivery boy who had been many times to her home said that she was the same nice person and she tipped generously. She achieved professionalism. She separated what she had to do, and which she doesn't judge, from her private life and her personal feelings. Lacking the conveniences of a clinical setting, she nevertheless did her job in a thoroughgoing fashion. I feel no anger toward this girl, Raymond. Why do you?"

Paternostra: "I'll tell you why he's angry, Albert. Raymond often speaks of being a father. *[Pause.]* I am suggesting that you not laugh again, Sebastian. This is only a suggestion, but it's the last one. Raymond has spoken of wheeling his baby in a carriage down Mohawk Street on a Sunday afternoon. This is who Raymond is in private, who none of you know, but I honor deeply, in spite of the crudity of his manner at times."

Cesso: "I see."

Spina: "Oh! Albert sees! But what do I see? I see a well-stacked young bull, Mr. Raymond Hudson of the West Coast, considered to be handsome in several quarters. This young man should get married, Joseph. Do you see me laughing? Then he can wheel the fucking carriage down Mohawk at midnight when the African-Americans take hold, as far as I'm concerned. That's it! I'm not laughing. What's so hard about that? You want to be a fucking father? God bless! Get married."

Ayoub: "And if he doesn't wish to be married? Or cannot get it up for marriage?"

"In this era, my friend? Don't make me laugh. There are women out there who want to be fucked hard into pregnancy but they don't want to get married either, because they have no shame, if that's what he wants out of life. Unless, of course *[Caught up now in the surge of his oratory, his Spina wit:]* He's some kind of queer!"

Spina breaks out into uncontrollable laughter. He's weeping. The others sit in silence, with the exception of Ayoub, who chuckles. Spina manages, just barely: "Imagine it! A tough young guy like him!"

Ayoub to the innocent Spina, raising his voice suddenly and harshly: "In other words, Joseph must also be one. Hilarious, Sebastian."

"Louis," Cesso says, "are you asking me to disrespect you? If this is your desire, I will try to satisfy it."

Spina, a Niagara of sweat: "He'll satisfy the professor! Albert's another one!"

"The fecund father of nine," Ayoub staring at Cesso, "who shits them out on a regular basis. His wife won't leave him alone."

Suddenly relaxed, almost sweet, Raymond says: "How about that! A roomful of faggots."

Robert: "We are perhaps all in the cellar. Am I wrong?"

Paternostra: "Mr. Forza, you're not wrong. We're all comfortable here in this place where children fear to come."

Raymond: "Maybe Professor Cunt wants me to knock him up, which is a vague feeling I'm having with my pistol in my hand ready to go off."

Paternostra: "Gentlemen, who are we? Who are we? Alex, I understand, has placed his daughter somewhere faraway after the tragedy of his life. He made a painful father's decision. Albert needs no introduction as a father. But I, me, Joseph Paternostra, and you Sebastian, and Raymond, and the Professor, and I must believe you too Mr. Forza: What are we all? We are childless. Or, as I prefer to say it: We are fathers without children, because we are always fathers, however unfulfilled. This is our truth."

Ayoub: "Who among us is a secret unfulfilled mother?"

Paternostra: "Is that such a bad thing, Professor, that you have to say it in that tone of voice? To want to be a mother? This person from the Parkway—"

Robert: "Her name?"

Ayoub: "She is in custody. That is all ye need to know."

Paternostra: "Because this name is a meaningless name, Mr. Forza. The meaning of this person is that she became a mother and then tried to unbecome a mother, which is her tragedy."

Cesso: "Yes."

Robert: "The tragic heroine decided not to hand over her baby to someone who would have wanted it."

Paternostra: "Raymond would have taken this baby."

Raymond: "Yes."

Cesso: "Yes."

Paternostra: "But the rest of us childless fathers? You, Sebastian, you who want to be this city's next Father?"

"I'm not married."

Paternostra: "But as you insisted concerning Raymond."

"I'm not that type of person."

Cesso: "Who in this world is the type? Not even Our Father in Heaven, when you consider what he put Our Lord through. Are you afraid to answer Joseph's question?"

"So I take the baby in because who can say no to a fucking little baby? Okay? That what you want to hear, Father Albert? Then what? Then I have this baby living in my own home. Okay? Since we're letting our hair down tonight I admit I can't handle the job. You don't want me as the father."

Cesso: "It's not possible for any man to handle the job. And it's not wrong to let one's hair down among friends, even Joseph should once in a while, which I've never witnessed in all of our years of close friendship. As his friend and medical advisor, his display of aggravation tonight—"

Paternostra: "What have I done to deserve this, Albert?"

Cesso: "Joseph?"

"That you should talk about me as if I were not in this room an arm's length away."

Raymond: "Choking distance."

Paternostra: "If it must be put that way."

Cesso: "Let your hair down for once, in view of your angina. Joseph, if the baby is offered to you, what do you do?"

"I would accept on Raymond's behalf. For myself, never. I'm not up to the job either."

Ayoub: "A child accepted on behalf of a person who is in effect your child, who will raise the child. You become a grandfather."

"Raymond is not my child. He is my friend, as you know."

"And the four young Italian-American studs who now make their names and small fortunes as the star chefs of this town? Who was their culinary father, Joseph?"

"I taught them, Professor."

"As your children or as your so-called friends?"

"I have no children, Professor."

Raymond: "He taught me how too. Joseph."

Ayoub: "Then these four young men are your deep friends?"

"They are my friends, Professor. Raymond is my deep friend, as you know. As for the four young men, I confess that I sometimes think of them as my sons. Often this thought comes strongly into me. But I have no sons. You, Professor? Would you have accepted the baby?"

"Better to have books than children. I have many books. They command my loving attention."

Raymond: "You wipe their bottoms?"

"I wipe their spines. Weekly. I have not yet so-called abused them, though it is my right as a parent. Actual children are an irritation, isn't that it, Joseph? Better to have these imitation sons of yours and mine."

"I have a few books, Professor, on the regions of Italian cuisine, but I give them almost no attention. Because a chef is from the mind. Many times, against my preference, I think of those boys as my sons. In the course of actual fatherhood, I imagine that there are many irritations. There must be. But underneath, unimaginable joy, I would imagine. For myself, I don't know the irritations or the joy. My feelings are bland on most things, though I consider myself somewhat fulfilled and a little raised up in the company of some young men who have been grateful for my small gifts."

Spina wants to know what Ayoub means when he says that if you're the parent it's your right to abuse your child, and Ayoub tells him it's not abuse, that Spina is making a "category mistake" and Spina replies, appalled, that "somebody has a mental problem and it's not me, Professor." Cesso disagrees, saying, "I think it's a philosophical point he's playing with," and Alex, still locked into his role as reverential student, adds, "He's going to explain why you don't go nearly far enough, Mr. Cesso, in your defense of the wretched girl who shall be unnamed." Robert, who's grasped Ayoub's literary allusion, says, "The Professor wishes, I believe, to make a modest proposal in order to reduce and perhaps even eliminate the awful crimes against children." Alex raises his hand and says, "In his ironical style."

Raymond: "He's sick."

Paternostra: "Mr. Forza, would you have accepted the child?"

"Whose child? Her name? Is this child to be forever nameless?"

Cesso: "The media says Jane Doe and Baby Doe, because of an ambiguity in the age. But the D.A. reserves the right to prosecute on a first-degree murder charge. We await the word of a higher court."

Robert: "But to people like yourselves, with connections, the name is known. Yes?"

Cesso: "Thanks to Sebastian."

"What is it?"

Cesso: "Mr. Forza, we have agreed beforehand to keep it from you, knowing that this is the sort of thing you need to know. We strongly suspect, we dearly hope that you saw us huddle. We huddled for your benefit, sir. We staged it. To whet your appetite."

"Why?"

Paternostra: "We intend to ensure completion of your secret history of this city. You love secrets. We have a few ourselves."

Cesso: "The name upon completion, Mr. Forza. Your power as the historian of our secrets is very great. But we, the audience, have power too."

"It is my pleasure to tell you stories. My pleasure is paramount."

Paternostra: "Unless it would give you the utmost pleasure to withdraw at the climactic moment."

Cesso: "Joseph has at last relaxed."

Ayoub: "Good. You have nothing to lose. Commence to narrate."

Paternostra: "But first Mr. Forza must answer. Would you have taken the newborn?"

Alex: "Then the Professor tells us his modest proposal."

"After which I weave again the threads of my Utica tale. My answer to you is Robert Forza abstains. To the offer of the newborn I say neither yes or no. A parent needs to be either female

or male. But I am neither here nor there. I throb between gen-
ders, blind, an old man with wrinkled female dugs, who's spent
his life wallowing in the waste of books. In memory of waste.
What do I know? Like you Professor Ayoub, I specialize in cruelty and am uniquely incapacitated for parenthood. As for my
vote on the wretched girl: I must abstain until such time as the
father is located, when I shall vote that Jane and John Doe be
summarily executed by the method with which they destroyed
their Baby Doe."

It occurs to Raymond that he may have found a new col-
league. He says, with perfect sincerity, "Where are we going to
find a toilet big enough? Time to eat." Then turns to the oven
and removes from it a truly massive thing, pie-like, thick and
smoking and more than twenty inches in diameter, its delicious
stuffing hidden between blankets of dough, olive oil smeared and
baked to a gleaming gold. The men, with the exception of
Paternostra, *il maestro,* grab in impulsive unison their forks and
knives. Robert, faster than all, has actually succeeded in inserting
his knife when Raymond says, "No, not for another half-hour,
until my flavors settle and mature." Joseph says, "We are indebted
to my good friend Professor Tommaso Stonato of Palermo, one
of those rare scholars whose practical achievements surpass his
exceptional erudition. The aroma of homemade pizza tends to
take our breath away, but the aroma of this! This is fatal. Because
this is not pizza. This is *Sfinciuni alla Siciliana.*" Raymond says, "I
slightly altered the original recipe, with Joseph's permission, to
make use of ingredients you can get here." Joseph says, "And
without loss of lethal impact, we can assure you." Raymond removes from the refrigerator two large bowls overflowing with a
green salad, saying, "In the meanwhile, let's tackle this and let's
drink some wine and toast the fathers who aren't."

And so they begin to work over the salad and the wine, but
can talk only (as Ayoub puts it) of "Raymond's big thing before
us." What is it, exactly, that we'll be eating? Would Raymond be

so kind as to afford us a little revelation as it cools, and as we are aroused? He would not. Good. Ayoub then will offer in substitution a brief historico-anthropological meditation on "this thing as it appears to us, this mysterious phenomenon bristling with hints of noumenal substance," claiming that though it was unfamiliar to them, he, Louis Ayoub, definitely recognized the genre, "the obvious Middle Eastern provenance," because what, after all, were the Sicilians culturally considered anyway? Or, for that matter, what were they considered from the genetic point of view? "Joseph, for example, is a Sicilian, and who, or what, is Joseph?" At which juncture, Robert interposes a doubt that a "worthy distinction" between the cultural and the genetic is available in the "advanced theoretical context" within which such questions "nowadays" were to be entertained. Ayoub says, "Yes, Mr. Forza. Sicily, that beautiful wasteland, has tantalized the great civilizations for centuries. Think of the long Arab domination of that wretched place, whose sterility, whose very dryness, is a provocation, the short skirt, as it were, and unrefusable challenge to the virility of invading cultures." Robert says, "And the invaders thought, 'Ah, but to make it moist! To inseminate Sicily. Were that possible, the whole world would then surely lie beneath our feet.' " Alex jumps in, "Laid 'neath the Imperial Penis?" And Ayoub replies, "Alex! 'A' plus plus!" "In other words," says Alex, "we do it in the dark. We eat in the dark. We make love in the dark." And Robert, hearing his cue at last, says, "What issues forth from the Sicilian womb? Or from any womb? What child is this?" Ayoub, staring at Paternostra: "And what rough beast is this?" To which Paternostra, with newfound quickness: "Or you, Professor? Who are you? Are you so sure of who you are? A thrilling suggestion, Alex. We'll eat it in the dark. Raymond! A candle!" But Raymond, of course, has no candle, and must ascend, to speak to John, who doesn't have one either, because why would he? John must call home, there will be a delay. But Paternostra will brook no delay.

He puts out the light and says, "We should accustom ourselves to the dark before we pick up our weapons. In the meantime, Professor, please amuse us with your modest proposal. How far do you go, Professor?" Ayoub replies that he's not adequate to the stylistic demands of his great Anglo-Irish predecessor, but "for sport" will state the blunt particulars. "One: We know that Albert is pro-life; Albert says that the Virgin Mary was not with tissue, but with child. Two: In addition, and paradoxically, Albert assents, as we've tonight heard for the first time, to the extremest form of the pro-choice position, doubtless in an effort to fuse the antagonists in a dialectical levitation of both. He wants the murdering mother to go free. Which leads us to point three and the heart of Albert's exquisite irony: a mother's right to choose to exterminate is equivalent to the right, hitherto unknown, to exterminate life itself, both *in utero* and *extra uterum,* both inside and outside the clinical setting, because setting is not the essence of the matter, because setting is merely the material circumstance of the act of free choice which must suffer no limitation. Four (a subpoint of three), the right to exterminate must perforce be extended *extra uterum,* because the first *(in utero)* is only a special instance of the principal that states that a mother's right to act upon the body of a child, from the point of inception, is not abridgeable. The life of the so-called *minor* is better understood as that of a *foetus.* The minor is nothing but a foetus. Five: A parent, therefore, has the right to exterminate her foetus at any time prior to the age of eighteen years and nine months, the full term of foetus life. The overarching principle here is that of the right to dispose of one's private property as one sees fit. Anything short of parental administration of immediate death to the foetus—say, punching, or kicking, or raping— . . . but I grow weary." Robert, eager to play literary nurse to Ayoub's faltering Jonathan Swift, says, "And may they not be sold to slaughterhouses? The foetuses? Butchered and distributed free to the homeless?" Ayoub, nodding in gratitude, says, "Yes. But I recommend bringing the child to the homeless alive, and dressing it hot to the knife, as we do roasting pigs. Yes, Raymond, I am sick."

A banging and a clattering is heard on the stairs beneath the trap door as John without a word, and guided by his flashlight from above, lowers in a metal bucket a single candle and candleholder, which Raymond fetches and at Paternostra's request carries not to the table but to the far corner to be lit. And then they go at it, with perfect geometry cutting themselves twelve-inch pie-like wedges. They go at it for a while in silence, only Spina offering a response to Ayoub's proposal for parental liberation: "I heard you were writing a book about hell, Professor." When well down the road to satiation, they begin to speak about this thing of Raymond's. What is this? Meatballs in here? Yes. Onions? Yes. Wine? Of course. I'm having trouble with a meat taste. Familiar but not familiar. Me too. Cat? Why not? And salami? Naturally. This is ricotta I'm eating? What do you think? But another kind of cheese besides? Yes. What is it? Guess. We can't figure it out. Too bad. Come on, Raymond. No. Joseph, what does this Sicilian word mean? *Sfinciuni.* Joseph tells them that it refers to a savoury meat pie sort of stuffed pizza, which tells them only what is obvious. Alex demands etymology. He turns to Ayoub. Robert says, "Etymology, sir, with poetic dimension. That is to say, etymology." And Ayoub says, "*Sfinciuni?* Consider *sfin,* out of the Greek signifying 'to draw tight'—and therefore to hide, make enigmatic, inscrutable. Whence *sphincter,* the powerful contractile muscular ring which keeps the anus normally closed and its contents hidden. Whence *sphinx,* mythical encloser or keeper of mystery. Finally *ciuni,* occurring solely in Sventuratu, the saddest sector of Sicily's remotest interior, the cultural dark side of the moon. *Ciuni:* orphan. Thus *sfinciuni:* child of the Sphinx, or child of the male womb, sprung by the Sphinxter, Keeper of Rectal Mystery. The ambiguity, I fear, is hopelessly fundamental.

Less poetically, we would say, simply, 'mysterious child,' which is widely accepted by advanced students of Sicilian culture."

Robert: "Chop extra fine and stir in Latin root of Italian *sfincio:* sponge. Hence, sponge-child. An orphan is a sponge whose function is to soak up the feelings of all those who dare to venture near it. Squeezed, it will express the feelings of others. In itself, the orphan is dry."

Raymond says: "Professor, I'm warming up to you. After all these years, I'm warming up."

———<>———

"Our fathers find their graves in our short memories, and sadly tell us how we may be buried in our survivors."

He pauses.

"We gather in desperate league against the opium of time."

Candle flickers, goes out.

"Is he starting?"

"Oh yeah."

"Fires? The destructions of our street signs? These are local manifestations only, however vivid and violent, of a general will to erase. We labor to beget and forget, and the diurnal murders of memory go unprosecuted. Bleecker, John, Rutger, Blandina, Mary, Lansing, Elizabeth, and Catherine: uprooted and defiled on the east side and in Utica's once elegant central district. Names of the early fathers and mothers, their daughters and sons, and a few favored in-laws: uprooted and defiled. Gentlemen, you would know the meaning? *[Raymond switches on electric bulb.]* A long-delayed, but inevitable declaration of war upon the founders and their descendants, and a surgical statement, directed to the Italians of Utica's east side, including those who have since moved on to the suburbs, to Florida, and to death. Who? Who would rename our streets? And where do we find the street signs honoring the names of the Italian pioneers? They gave us one. Just one.

Pellettieri Ave, a filthy and narrow passage, two short blocks in length, and they called it an avenue, without our consultation or assent. In mockery of the giants of our blood, they said let's call this ridiculous thing an avenue, and we accepted. We bowed. We bent over. When in floods the fathers of our fathers came over late in the last century, and in the early years of this dying one, Utica's streets had long been named. Now when in droves they leave, now how they flee us! The descendants of our ancestors! And the new surges of ethnic pressure would destroy the markers of this city's first fathers and replace them with markers of themselves. We say barbarism. We say madness. We say animals. Because we are afraid. We hear the scream and the screech of history's latest sharp turn of reason, and we hide behind words. They would rename the streets. Yes yes. Burn the classic neighborhood of the first fathers. And yet they persist, the first fathers continue to have their day. They will not go gently. How long have our addresses preserved their memories, when we would not? Our addresses? The graffiti of the fathers, the fathers' bulwark against the ingratitude of memory. The citizens of a new Utica would rebaptize the streets, the schools, the parks. They wish to write new graffiti all over this city: 'We are here. We were here.' To the future they would say, 'Speak our names daily, and thoughtlessly, as if the names of natural things, as you now say Bleecker and Rutger, mountains and rivers.' Graffiti over graffiti. The history of Utica is encoded in the palimpsest of graffiti, but the trace writing of the Italian-Americans, our own graffiti, where is it? The Italians of Utica were properly pronged by those who came before, and those who came long after us now wish to repeat the act. And they shall succeed. By both ends of history, we shall have been pronged. But I get ahead of myself."

"Properly?"

"We deserve it?"

"We deserve it. Yes. From Governor William Cosby to Rutger Bleecker, to you, Mr. Spina."

"An assassination here and there, a little political pressure, a lot of liberal guilt, and they get a couple of streets. Tops."

"We gave them Martin Luther King Drive."

"They want O. J. Simpson Boulevard."

"Mr. Forza, the idea of wholesale renaming is absurd."

Silence.

"They would rename the city."

Burst of derision.

"Mr. Paternostra, your thinking is narrowed in the blood of your immigrant heritage. Some come as immigrants, the needy grateful come as immigrants, but others come as if none had come before. Explorers. Imperialists sometimes in deed, but always in desire. They are the strong. They are the namers, and the namers are always new, as if the land were always virgin. The strong say, 'Let us here make a settlement, and let it be called New Amsterdam. The world is Dutch.' The adventure over—when the baptismal rite is concluded the adventure is over—and the strong commence to bicker and feed upon each other and soon give way to the stronger, who say, 'Now it shall be called New York. The world is English. Let us settle ourselves upon the settlers.' Somebody came, and somebody already was here. Can you doubt my reasoning? Whole countries are renamed as we speak. It is the oldest of stories."

"Utica becomes New Saigon."

"This state becomes Outer Zimbabwe."

"In 1734, this entire valley was named Cosby Manor. Cosby's memory is preserved now by what? By something called Cosby Road. A farce. Cosby Road is a road in the same way that Pellettieri Ave is an avenue."

"On behalf of Mr. Forza's theory," says Ayoub, "we should inform him that the first of the street signs reported to have come down was none other than Cosby Road, which is nowhere near the central district or the east side. So I agree. Someone wants to make a major historical point."

Ayoub chuckles.

Ayoub says, "Was it you Mr. Forza? Are you the serial sign killer?"

No one laughs.

"A man of my physique?"

Everyone laughs.

"But this I must acknowledge, Professor. My heart in hiding stirs in sympathy. The new namers have arrived. The explorers are here and the period of general destructiveness is merely transitional. It is prelude to a new order. Surely thoroughgoing urban renewal is at hand."

"What place do we have in this order?"

"'We,' Mr. Cesso?"

"The Italian-Americans who have elected to stay. I apologize to Raymond and Alex for saying 'we.' But we are still the single largest group in Utica."

" 'We,' Mr. Cesso, are out. We've become classic, in a minor sort of way. We created a small genre of the classic mode. The major classic genre of naming was not found to be hospitable to our talents, such as they are. We never possessed the great stone mansions. They possessed us. The hospitals and the parks never bore our names, and never will. We'll be remembered as the people who added the genre of Mediterranean color to American history in its classic phase and can be identified now only on Columbus Day, as those who wear buttons saying, Kiss Me, I'm Italian. The Jews of America have disappeared. Looked for, they can be much found in their books. The Italian-Americans simply disappear. This is a good thing. You think this a grievous affair? This is a very good thing."

Paternostra: "Who are you, Mr. Forza?"

"Ah."

Paternostra: "Alex Lucas, who we trust, has represented you as his house guest. A so-called visitor to our city. Without casting stones on Alex, I have my doubts."

"Because you speak too familiarly," Ayoub says, "of this town and its past. No one who is not *Uticensis,* as Caesar said of Cato— of or belonging to Utica—could sustain such curiosity. It would be a true perversion."

"We checked you out, Mr. Forza. No such name in this town going back over fifty years. No such name. Who are you?"

"Mr. Hudson, I am the chronicler of an ancient civilization. I am the chronicle. In the classical world, a culture might reign for a thousand years. In America, things go very quickly. Here we eat cultures for breakfast and three hours later defecate them into the dark. The first commercial telegraph company in the world? Utica, 1846. By the turn of this century, we had become the textile center of the world! Utica Utica! They spoke so excitedly in the 1860s of New York, Boston, and Utica. They were totally beside themselves with excitement. In the 1850s and 1860s, thanks to men who survive themselves now as the names of drug-infested primary schools, all political mandates of both parties emanated from Utica. We were the mother. The first Woolworth store? Here because the cultural logic was irresistible. In Utica! Of Utica! The *Britannica Atlas* lists eight Uticas in the United States. The *Britannica* proper permits entry only to two: The first and glorious Utica of the ancients, on the coast of North Africa. And ours. The Utica of the eighth century before Christ; the Utica of the ancient Americans. Was. Were. Utica two is now also classical. In a minor sort of way. Our power and prestige lasted less than a century. We lose population now more rapidly than any comparable city in the country. How they flee her! They flee the dead land! We have the country's lowest bond rating and highest per capita consumption of pasta, the Italian contribution. And in the frenzy of his fame, oh yes! he stopped here on his American tour, he needed to see Utica, where his wit finally failed him. He, Oscar Wilde, reduced to stuttering sincerity, said: 'This. This. This, then, is Utica.' You wish to know who I am? I am the child whose father took him up one fine summer day to the northern high point of this valley, a child of perhaps five, and the father pointed to the gold dome of the Utica Savings Bank, gold in all that green, and the child said, 'Daddy, what is that?' And the daddy said, 'Robert, that is a very very big piece of chocolate all wrapped up in gold leaf.' And the child said, 'Let's go there.' "

Spina: "What happened to William Cosby and Rutger Bleecker? I'll be on my death bed before you get to that."

Raymond: "What's your real name."

"Irrelevant."

Paternostra: "As you sit there dying, Sebastian, how old are you exactly? Try not to tell me. I am ninety."

Spina: "This puts you slightly above the average Utica age."

"He saw it even then, in 1732, the first of our first fathers, William Cosby, he saw the bank with the chocolate dome wrapped in gold leaf in the midst of this wild Mohawk country. More than 20,000 acres in a rich valley, where the traffic flowing north from downstate turns west with the river. On his death bed, he, our most corrupt and avaricious of colonial governors, inside a circle of corruption he stood high, dripping, and he foresaw the Erie Canal, and the railroad, and this place, crossroads of commerce. He foresaw the nineteenth century. He who had worked hand in glove with the great colonial families of New York, giving them massive tracts of land, millions of acres for a song, in return for fat fees and political support, said, Now it's my turn. I want greatness for my family. We must be worshipped in books. That is my last wish. Let the books do the work of purifying my corroded life."

Ayoub: "Behind every great family lies a crime."

Paternostra: "And a politician."

Alex: "And eventually a writer."

"He was rich, he was powerful, he was dying. He regarded it as his duty to found his name, to thrust its piling deep into the new world. He said, 'And it shall be called Cosby Manor.' But the law stood in his way."

Alex: "The what?"

Raymond: "The law."

Paternostra: "The law."

"By 1732, the law said that an individual speculator could purchase only 2,000 acres, which does not a manor make. With the aid of ten dummy partners, he bought it all."

"They signed their deeds over to him?"

"Yes."

"Why?"

"He must have had something on them."

"No one knows the facts."

"They were dummies."

"What about the Indian claims?"

"Ha."

"In the beginning, it was just a few whites in ships. And the virgins, the Indians of Manhattan, said, Let us invent the theater of the awestruck primitive. Ha. Let these eighty-three white children have Manhattan. It's a small thing, and the world is red. We'll take the gaily colored cloth. The glass beads too. Because they saw in the beads and the cloth economic leverage over tribes that they had long wished to devour. Red meat for red meat, said the First American Eaters. The first people of Manhattan even felt pangs of guilt for taking advantage of the fat white children. By 1732, in the colony of New York, they'd become stooges of imperial cunning. *[Pause.]* A few rifles, the right to hunt and fish at will, rum and beer. The Dutch breweries of the Bleeckers worked overtime. Cosby paid the crown for the acreage bought, and paid yearly rent. So the governor had his Cosby Manor. At his death it existed. But he did not foresee, as the great never do, the small-mindedness, the pettyness of his heirs. Starting with the wife."

Ayoub: "They said why should we pay taxes to the crown etcetera. We want our freedom etcetera."

"Yes. That is what they said. They said revolution etcetera. It was the cloak of fashion among those great Hudson River families.

Freedom and so forth. They did not wish to pay. Not even a tiny amount."

Ayoub: "Without representation etcetera."

Paternostra: "And who could blame the families? I've always resented having to pay."

Ayoub: "And you don't. Not even for a cup of coffee at Caruso's. You expect Carmen to give it to you free. Behind every great fortune there is a crime. That's how they get rich. They make someone else pay."

Alex: "Balzac, Prof, on the old world great families."

Ayoub: "Remembered by Mario Puzo in the epigraph to *The Godfather*. Behind every great fortune there is a crime. Remembered in linkage of all the great families, legitimate and illegitimate, in the womb of crime, the United States of the Mafia. All wealth is guilty at the source."

Paternostra: "The Professor overexaggerates everything."

Ayoub: "The road of exaggeration leads to the palace of fact."

"Yes, the homeopathic imagination of Mario Puzo, the splendid luridness of his instincts, whose ancestors hid the meaning of their surname by dropping the second 'z.' Mario the novelist with a nose for the disguised stench of all great families. Puzo? *Puzzo:* Stink. Cosby in his grave had long passed the stage of putrefaction when forty years after death and the quitrents on Cosby Manor long in arrears and the heirs refusing to pay and thinking they were immune because too well connected to the provincial powers, because hadn't they intermarried with the other great families? Back and forth, back and forth the intermarriages went, all cousins now, fornicating in each other's bedrooms, so why should they, the heirs, fear that their cousin Philip Schuyler—"

"Who?"

"He just brought in a new dramatic person."

"Related to our very own Schuyler Corners?"

"Oh yeah. That's his graffiti."

"This very Philip, who is now reduced to a sign at the northeastern rural corners of Utica, whom French dignitaries had admired as one of the most considerable men in America, altogether irresistible, they said, who would become a hero of the revolution, so how should they, the Cosby heirs, guess that he, cousin Philip, would conspire with three other men, including Rutger Bleecker, the big-bottomed brewmeister of Albany who was himself a cousin among the cousins, one of the resistible ones licking the wounds to his self-esteem in the corner, whose family (Rutger's), the Bleeckers of the original Dutch settlers, who were wealthy, yes, but not overwhelmingly so—not like a Schuyler, or a Livingston, or a Van Renssaeler, because they were just Bleeckers: booze makers, mayors, aldermen, church deacons, Indian so-called interpreters, and chief suppliers of the jolly groggeries of Albany County with specialization in easing the grief at funerals, who had so many times their kettles distrained by the sheriff for illegally supplying alcohol to the Indians they were interpreting for the governors and the merchants and the land jobbers—"

"Hey! Slow down!"

"Why are you all of a sudden going so fast without hardly breathing? We don't want to be thrown for a loop. We want a story."

"His face is getting redder by the second."

"He's entered the Faulknerian phase of his narrative style."

"And what is that, Professor Ayoub? Speak in English."

"He's panting for the past. He's a necrophiliac. He's hot for the dead. He's going out of control in the ecstasy of—"

"But they—"

"Who?"

"The Bleeckers. The Bleeckers had no manor either until Philip Schuyler conspired with old Roger the Bleacher—"

"Who?"

"The meaning of Rutger Bleecker: Roger the Bleacher, the Whitener, who Philip allowed to think that he, Rutger, could rename Cosby Manor in honor of his, Roger's family, because he, Philip, had a manor, because Philip was interested only in a Mohawk country extension of himself—he had many extensions and he only wanted to insert his finger a little bit into the Mohawk—"

"Philip the Fingerfucker."

"Philip had many very nice tracts spread all over the state but he had no Mohawk and he wanted to cover the state because he could no longer acquire the one sublime tract—500,000 dummy partners were not a possibility—one spread sublime enough to astonish the future, impossible, so he wanted to make the name of Schuyler inevitable, he was here and he was there with his finger. He wanted the future to think Schuyler every time it heard New York. At 9:00 A.M. on the Fourth of July, in 1772, Cosby Manor was to be auctioned. Philip and his partners arrived at the Albany marketplace at 8:45. At 8:55, they, the sole bidders, bought Cosby Manor for fifteen cents per acre. The sheriff was supposed to auction off only enough to pay the arrearage. But he sold it all. It is not said in the history books why the auction started early, or why they were the only bidders, or why the sheriff sold the entire manor. When the heirs of Cosby, the cousins, were told the news, they became bananas—"

"*Went* bananas, Robert."

"All the cousins who were the heirs spoke to each other and then to cousins Philip and Rutger. Only into Philip, who had a major, major reputation to protect, were they able to insert pressure."

"*Apply* pressure, Robert."

"But Bleecker the big-bottomed was not to be moved. He had licked too long in the shadows. Schuyler, broken-hearted, after a year of internecine negotiation, his Mohawk country initiative decisively thwarted, gave back to the heirs a huge portion of what he'd bought. Then the Revolution, etcetera. No more landed aristocrats. Bleecker, in sympathy, wishing to spare cousin Philip the agony of further involvement in his blasted dream, sent his (Rutger's) son John, in 1786, to survey Cosby Manor."

Alex: "To thrust his own piling deep."

Raymond: "Right into cousin Philip and those other two guys."

Cesso: "The history of our city is the history of land swindles?"

Paternostra: "It's a free country, people take initiative on their own behalves. After all, this is not Europe. When they don't take initiative, they take welfare. I personally never took welfare."

Ayoub: "You personally took something, Joseph."

Spina: "I can't go along with running down America, it's a shame, which is what I think you're saying since last night, Mr. Forza, though you have every right to say it, which is the reason why we go to war every generation."

Ayoub: "Mario the Stinker has already told your story of swindlers, Mr. Forza, and made a fortune doing so."

Robert: "As did Mr. Faulkner before him."

Ayoub: "Yes."

Robert: "As did Mr. Fitzgerald before Mr. Faulkner."

Ayoub: "Yes. The American literary history of family gangsterism."

Robert: "America as the history of land swindling from day one."

Ayoub: "It's obvious."

Robert: "It's obvious. But I have not told you this story."

Cesso: "Tell us, Mr. Forza, what did you tell us?"

Robert: "The teller does not tell about the telling. He can only tell himself banally."

Alex: "We would say, Is that all there is, Mr. Forza?"

Spina: "These big shots you go on about, they're nobodies. They were big once, but so what, frankly? Until you mentioned it last night, I never knew that Bleecker was the name of a person.

Who thought about it? Who gave it a thought is my point? Blandina, Catherine, Elizabeth. Family members? Blandina was a person?"

Robert: "Yes, female. A Bleecker."

Cesso: "Here today, gone tomorrow. But Our Lord does not forget."

Raymond: "Neither does Joseph."

Ayoub: "All is vanity. Feedeth the wind, la la."

Cesso: "Is that supposed to be false, Louis?"

Ayoub: "In the archeological digs, they find signs broken off their posts, bearing words. Rutger. Bleecker. They attempt to relate these words to other words preserved on tin cans and on fragments of glass and in a few thousand battered books. They do not know that the words are signs. They're not confident that the words are proper names. They put these words in new books in which they perform speculative feats of linguistics, philological leaps among the dusty shards of a culture."

Robert: "Ages hence they may say of this word 'Utica,' our Utica, what today's scholars say of the ancient Utica of the Phoenicians, located in what we are now pleased to call Tunisia. Unknown. Origin and coinage unknown. I feel that such a state of affairs should not be viewed as tragic. I am attempting to resist a powerful feeling that wants me to say that this state of affairs is a very deep good. The deepest of goods, perhaps."

Ayoub: "For the architect of the pyramids, whose name is unknown, we need have no pity. Let us not commit the crime of geneology constructed and remembered."

Cesso: "Mr. Forza, please help me. You began by indicting the murderers of memory. You said, 'The general will to erase.' Now you are telling us that we're doing the dead a favor? Why do you wish to know the wretched girl's name, if not to give a name to the dead newborn, who you don't want to be nameless? I'm confused."

Alex: "Not even a dusty shard for that baby."

Paternostra: "Albert isn't the only one who's confused."

Ayoub: "That baby went into the big night of time without a name. The big nothing."

Raymond: "Also into the small day of time without one."

Robert: "Mr. Hudson is not confused."

Alex: "A little recognition by the parents is required."

Cesso: "A little care."

Ayoub: "In the brief light."

Paternostra: "Give a little living room to the living."

Alex: "Push out the dead. Write all over them. Renew the city, what I say."

Cesso: "At least wait until we're dead at least."

"It's too easy to give a shit about the dead."

"To weep for them."

"Easy."

"Better to read your phone book."

"Memorize it in high school. Forget Shakespeare."

"The unknown living. Pronounce their names alphabetically."

"Womb to toilet."

"Weep for them, they live."

"He's confused."

"I'm not confused, gentlemen."

"Yes you are."

"Mr. Forza is big with significance."

"In its small life, it meant nothing to nobody in this world."

"Who?"

"Forza is anything you want him to be."

"Who?"

"Then he's nobody."

"What was its gender?"

"I think that I may be somebody. I am perhaps a person who requires dessert after all major meals. Mr. Hudson? Will you disappoint me again, as you did last night, when I was forced to retire dessertless?"

Raymond is happy. He likes the high-toned style in which he is addessed. No one has ever called him Mr. Hudson in quite that way. He brings to the table seven slabs of chocolate gelato. "Compliments of Caruso's," he says. "Carmen heard you were going to be here, Lucas. He says to me, 'This kid is terrific.' I say, 'He's not going to eat seven, Carmen.' Carmen says, 'Consider yourselves lucky to be in his company.'" Spina says, "I think this town is on the verge of an era of good feeling."

<hr>

"The cruel spring of 1798, and six more years to pass before his death, when the citizens of this place, yet called Old Fort Schuyler, gathered to bury the man alive whose name their village bore, and whose status as a romantic character of Revolution was quite fresh. The forty or so adult males decided, after much inconclusive debate, to write their choices of a new name on slips of paper. The slips placed in a hat. The name written by the lawyer and classical scholar, Erastus Clark, drawn and Utica baptized on the third of April, 1798."

"Sounds like he's giving a funeral speech."

"About a baptism."

"We need a little color and background on this Clark."

"The details of Clark do not survive."

"We've waited long enough. When do we get to our obscure Italian fathers? Give us everything you have about John Marchisi and Alessandro Lucca."

"Not tonight."

A voice from over the trap door: "Eventually, I have to go home."

"Wrap it up, Mr. Forza."

"Close the coffin."

"Utica: a Latin translation and transliteration of a Phoenician word now lost, they say. Not to be found among the inscriptions. Lost to the scholars, given to us. We know this: the ancient Utica of 800 years before Christ was the oldest of the Phoenician settlements in North Africa. Older than Carthage. Why did they choose that place for the first place, those fabulous merchants, if not for need of a port from which they could proceed with ease, with their wares to Sicily, less than 200 miles away, and then beyond? A port. A place of entry, yes. But egress to those ancient merchants, it was egress, it was always egress that was of the essence. Egress like *utterance,* in its most obsolete and profoundest sense: a mouth, a place of emission, an outlet. A port of communication. The *ut* of utterance, that from which utterance itself emerges. *Ut* as the first note in the diatonic scale, that from which other notes may be said to proceed, yes yes to utter is to put forth to issue to eject to bring to light—"

"Hey! Slow down!"

"The corpse of Latin moves."

"And isn't it odd that the Latin *utique,* meaning without qualification, *necessarily*, is the same as the French *Utique*, which is what they now call old Utica in Tunisia today?"

"Can it be far behind, Mr. Forza, the *ut* of uterus?"

"Yes, Professor Ayoub, the uterus which our fantastic ancestors in the ancient world thought to be the cavity which is not controlled by your *sphinxter,* because it is the womb of the earth itself, out of which the first creatures were born. The original place of egress. Ut Ut. They, the Phoenicians, called their first city, in North Africa, Carthage, a word found in the inscriptions. Carthage. New City. First City. But Carthage came after Utica. Utica was not a city. Utica was first before the first city, it was original, it was the origin, as the uterus is first, the necessary port. The uterus is *inside,* gentlemen. It yields and yields to the outside until it can yield no more. It becomes depleted. From the proto-

Semitic, which I neither pronounce or write there is a word that sounds like the sounds of simultaneous coughing and spitting up, and it means the first place, and that sound which I myself cannot utter but have heard uttered from an unusually gifted reference librarian is the sound of Utica, if you were saying Utica at the same time that you were gagging and coughing up your phlegm, hawking it out, you would be saying this sound which I cannot utter—a sound akin to an utterance in Hebrew: to advance from, to proceed, and in its substantive form: a weaned child."

"They considered that the first thing they had to have on the North African coast was a uterus. In honor of their mothers."

"Yes."

"From which they could send out—"

"Obviously."

"From which they could express—"

"Press out, Raymond."

"Their utterances."

"Their stuff."

"Their rugs."

"Their kids. Weaned."

"Eventually she dries up."

"Utterly."

"Udderly."

"The womb dies. Utica dies."

"Then what, Mr. Forza?"

"Then we have the unfulfilled fathers without children. Who cannot father children. We have the end."

"The sphinxter opens. It permits egress."

"They birth their shit. The fathers."

"They?"

"We birth our shit."

"Including the wretched girl of the Parkway. Who moved her bowels."

"For which you shouldn't get arrested."

"Then we have the end."

"The adult males in 1798 pulled out of a hat—"

"Out of the womb of chance."

"They pulled from the womb of chance the word of the womb, which is not the womb."

"We have the end."

"I think we have the end."

As they leave Joe's, they notice it: yanked up and lying in the gutter. The street sign for Pellettieri Ave.

Chapter 9

He returns, after a night elsewhere, to find Robert standing in the middle of the office. Robert says, "Welcome home, Romeo." Alex smiles and blushes. Robert says, "He's dead." Alex says, "Somebody died? Who died?" Robert's eyes are like fish eyes. He replies, "Morris Reed." Alex says, "I don't know the name." Robert says, "I've just told you the name. You mean that you cannot link the name with a person you have seen. Or with significant deeds. Now you know a name that refers to nothing." Alex responds, "That about covers it." Robert says, "He covered me many times when I was a child, when I went to bed. This man who acted as if he were my father. Who did the deeds of a father. Morris. Morris Reed. Unlike you. Who are a biological father, but do not do the significant deeds. You are a father in your thoughts alone." Alex says, "And by his deeds you may be defined as his son. Which you didn't say. Why didn't you say it? I'm going to make a pot of coffee. Come on up."

As they sit in Alex's kitchen, Robert tells him everything. When he's finished, Alex says, "You're telling me in February of 1954 you buried a baby in Spina's backyard? And you never told anyone about it until now? You didn't worry someone would notice the fresh upturned earth?"

"The shed was never used."

"I have news for you. There is no shed. No garden. No cherry tree. It's all blacktop. Why didn't you tell anyone at the time?"

"It would have done no good."

"How deep did you dig?"

"A narrow trench, perhaps two-feet deep. Then old boards and automobile junk piled on top of the dirt. To make her safe from burrowing animals."

"And from the blacktoppers. *[Pause.]* Forty-two years ago."

"A jar. A scarf. A delicate skeleton."

"No reports of missing children. No kidnappings."

"A secret affair of the family."

"The raccoons were in hibernation. In that type of cold spell, even the possums and the crows hunker down, or they would have eaten it on Albany Hill."

"It? Her. She."

"Safe in the ice. Any footprints?"

"One set. Boots probably. But no distinguishing characteristics."

"You took it upon yourself to—"

"Yes."

"At eighteen years old."

"Yes."

"A few months later you leave these people, the Reeds, without a trace. Without giving notice. You've told me almost nothing about your times with them."

"I can't remember, really. How much do you remember of your parents, in truth? How much could you actually write out, if asked? Let's be honest. Forty-two years from now, what would you remember of your first eighteen years with them? I mean, in terms of sentences, how many could you write down that would actually describe in vivid detail your interactions with them? What they literally said and did? What were they wearing? The colors. The food on the plate. How many sheets of paper would be required? *Remember,* not invent. How much do we know about them before they were married? Who are these people, our parents, really?"

"These people raised you. That's who they are. What significant deeds did you do that would define you as the son? Then you disappeared. You burrowed underground. Then you came back."

"I've already told you. Why repeat?"

"Describe in one fairly short, but vivid, sentence some of your sonlike behavior."

"I can't. Not even in my thoughts was I a son."

"You're probably black. Now that you tell me about your background, you're starting to look black to me in your features. In a subtle way, you're obviously black. On the other hand, you're obviously not. Do you grieve for this man who acted like your father, but wasn't?"

"I was going to see him again today, for the third time in three days. To tell him that it didn't disturb me that he berated me mercilessly. I enjoyed it, in fact. I would have told him. I wanted to request the freedom to drop in on him on a weekly basis. Without notice. This is how I saw our future. For perhaps thirty-five minutes per session. A time brief enough to protect us both. And would he permit this, please, in the context of a friendship, not a kinship? We could talk. But I could not behave as a son. On that score, my friend, I could cut him no slack. When I arrived, I found Darryl Crouse sitting on the top step in front of Morris's door. A teenager who lives on the first floor. His eyes were puffy and red. He told me later that he was eighteen. When I left, he told me, 'I'll miss him in the future.' A white boy by the name of Darryl Crouse heard a crash on the stairs and ran up to the third floor to find Mr. Reed face down on the stairs, groceries everywhere, a broken bag of spaghetti. Under his face, on the stairs, blood. He must have hit his nose, Darryl said, and was knocked out from the fall. Darryl called nine eleven. They worked on him and then they said he was dead. A coronary of tremendous impact. Dead before he smashed his nose, at about eight this morning, falling through the air already dead, still holding the grocery bag. I arrived at ten. Now it's almost noon and Morris is at the morgue, which I will not visit. Alex, the detail of the spaghetti interested me. I was skeptical until I found a piece of penne. Darryl called it spaghetti when I showed him. He said, 'I missed that one when I cleaned up.' In my teen years, Morris refused to eat pasta. All of my talk about Gregorio and Caterina Spina infuriated him. He would have no signs of them in his house. At the time, he hated the Spinas, though he never met them. He called them slaveholders. Darryl Crouse gave the police the envelope that Morris asked him to pass on in case of an emergency, in which he was rendered silent for whatever reason. Darryl said the letter said that Morris wanted combustion. The money for it was in the envelope in hundred dollar bills. He wanted Darryl to have the ashes."

"Who's this Darryl Crouse to him?"

"The boy that he'd taken to lunch once a week for the last seven years, according to Darryl Crouse. Every Saturday. Darryl lives with his mother."

"Now you want the ashes."

"No. I haven't earned the ashes. I wish to purchase a proper urn. Where does one purchase an urn of a classical aspect?"

"You just decided to disappear into New York City?"

"I didn't decide. I left the way any eighteen-year-old might leave, in search of some vague but thrilling new life. When I saw the room in the bookstore, a life among books presented itself to me. It beckoned, an actual whole life, real not vague, physical as well as mental, among books. I was sucked in deep, and then I decided. I must have wanted to lose myself, or so we say retro-spectively. I cut off all contact with the Reeds, who could only remind me of my meaninglessness, which is how we see it now. I have no recollection, none, of what I was thinking when I cut myself off. A gross sentimentality, perhaps the grossest, to think, now, that I was actually capable at that time of thinking. That I had a logic, an intention. I found myself disappearing into the new place. I liked the feeling. What else is there to say? Then set about to read every book I could find about the old place and how it came to be. Now I've returned to realize a wish of my childhood. To be a black Italian on Mary Street."

"No one will know that you're black. Not even you know for certain."

"The urns, Alex?"

"Heather has several beauties. They look old."

"When do we close on 1303 Mary Street?"

"About three weeks."

"I can't wait that long."

"Ten days. I can do ten days."

"Put it all in your name."

"You nuts?"

"You will kindly permit me to live there rent free."

"The check in my account. The home in my name. What is this? Dickens?"

"Do you own this house?"

"This dump? It's been in the family for years."

"You have it free and clear?"

"Yes."

"Good. The check in your account. Two houses of your own free and clear. Because this is Dickens and I need to unScrooge myself. You will bring a material base of your own into the rapidly developing relationship with Heather Faxton."

"She's not the type to hold it over me."

"I speculate that you're the type."

"There's a body in Spina's backyard? A body!! You going to just leave it there after you move in?"

"A skeleton. Of course I will leave it there. What else? I have two goals, Alex. We must find a way to destroy Spina's mayoral candidacy and we must find a way to convince the people in the stronghold of far eastern Mary Street that they have a nigger in their midst."

"Bullshit."

"How now?"

"The nigger speech. Twice in three days. More or less word for overblown word. You know what you remind me of when you talk about yourself as a nigger? An actor who forces the big moment. From what you told me, you loved those people on Mary Street when you were a kid, and they were crazy about you. You wanted to live there? Why? You still want to live there. It's obvious. It was your idea of having a home where you saw yourself happy, instead of where you were. The nigger speech belongs to Morris Reed. The man whose nose bled into the pasta this morning, but who refused to eat pasta when you were a kid in order to make a point. Here's a question for you, Robert. What do you know about Morris Reed, in truth? *Know*, not invent. Here's another one. Do you grieve for this man? Are you grieving?"

"What is grief?"

"Give me a break."

"You grieved for Caroline, apparently. Tell me what it was like. We'll compare our respective affective states. I assume you grieved for her, even though your report on her death scene was thickly coated with rage. Perhaps you would like to remove your coat? *[Pause.]* Rage is superficial. *[Pause.]* Rage is the surface of sadness, and sadness is without bottom."

"She said . . ."

"What did she say, Alex?"

"'Am I going to die, Alex?'"

"What did you answer?"

"I said, 'This is routine. Don't worry about it.'"

"Was she reassured?"

"She started drifting in and out. Someone said the words stage one coma. One of the nurses tapped her cheek a few times. Caroline rubbed her tummy. She said, 'I'm six weeks pregnant.' She drifted. She said, 'Leave me alone.'"

"After, did you cry?"

"I yelled. Caroline was diabetic, but that didn't scare her. She wanted one bad. The doctor said that the diabetes had nothing to do with it, Mr. Lucas, 'I can assure you. Your baby is 100 percent healthy. Catastrophic postpartum hemorrhage,' she said, 'is rare, unpredictable, and unstoppable in virtually every case. In these times, the risks for a diabetic pregnancy are almost as low as for a normal uncomplicated one, if your wife took care of herself, which she did beautifully. The diabetes had no impact, Mr. Lucas.' I said if she didn't have the baby she'd be alive. You know what the doctor said when I said that? 'Mr. Lucas, this is true.' Then I yelled. I cried."

"Did the doctor comfort you?"

" 'You're a man, Mr. Lucas, and you love your wife.' *[Pause.]* Later she told me that I'll never get over it and in the long run this is a very good thing. Never to get over it. 'It is human never to get over it, Mr. Lucas. Why should you get over it? Are you a machine?'"

"This morning, Alex, I neither yelled nor cried. According to your lady doctor, my manhood is in question. Am I a man, Alex?"

Alex feels devilish. He says, "This is routine. Don't worry about it." They laugh. Robert says, "Am I going to die, Alex?" They laugh, harder.

Alex says, "Something dawns on me. The last thing that Morris told you was that he was your father. You took it as one of his merciless jokes. After all, he raised you, is all he was saying. Stop looking. Because here I am. The male person who brought you up, who loved you, I am your father in that sense. But maybe he was saying, 'I am your father in every sense, including genetically.' Think about it. Those stories of they didn't know where they carried you from, where you were handed over etcetera. He can't remember the town, or he won't tell you the town, or the people's names. That's ridiculous, maybe. Because maybe it was all made up. Because that was the condition laid down by his wife. Morris Reed actually had an affair with a white woman. An Italian. Why not? He wanted the baby he couldn't have with Aunt Melvina. She always wanted one too but couldn't stomach your particular production route. So she laid down the condition, the preposterous story of adoption, because the condition was that Morris could never say to you, I am your true father. He could be a father in every way except those words could never be spoken by him to you. That was the price of infidelity. This would explain Morris's bitter rage toward the Spinas, with you going on about the Spinas day and night, you're breaking his heart in such a tremendous way it's unfathomable how bad it must have been for him. That's my theory."

"And a very cruel theory it is, Alex."

"If you had come back from New York after a few silent months, they would have been so happy that they would have told you the truth. This is theoretical."

"Would you be so kind as to pick up the ashes tomorrow morning at 11:00 and bring them here for safe keeping? Crown Hill Memorial Park, Incorporated. Perhaps you will consult Heather, on my behalf, and Darryl's, concerning a proper urn."

"I can do these things."

"Eighteen hundred degrees of purification for two-and-a-half hours. The glory of God is a devouring fire. The skeleton is then put through a pulverizer. The glory of man reduces the bones to an appearance of crushed sea shells. Alex, did the Professor teach you Sir Thomas Browne's *Urn Burial*?"

"He taught us Joyce's *Ulysses*. Womb-tomb."

"Mr. Joyce is very good. Womb-tomb is very very good. A brilliant effect, though somewhat diminished by its reliance on a rhyming accident of the English language. A happy accident, uniting our beginning and our end. But Sir Thomas had a superior insight, dependent on no accident of language, bound to no language of this world, and therefore universal. A deep structure. He pointed out that the common form of the cinerary urn duplicates the form of the uterus, thereby making our last bed like our first. Art imitates nature, and nature is its own excuse for being."

"We leave the urn of the uterus by moving down through the neck and into the world. Down the birth canal. Down into the world."

"We stay in the bowl of the urn. We are not required to leave our last bed. *[Pause.]* Call Mr. Paternostra and tell him that I am unable to make an appearance this evening. The show will not go on."

"What reason should I give?"

"No reason."

"When do we reschedule? What if they ask?"

"Tell them that they will be given ample notice. Tell them that next time kid must be prepared."

"What if I ask you, privately?"

"Ask me what, Alex?"

"Why you canceled. Why can't you go on, Robert?"

Silence.

"Do you grieve?"

Silence.

"Robert?"

"Am I yelling? Am I crying?"

"Do you grieve, Robert?"

Robert rises, walks to wall. Back to Alex, hands clasped behind back, staring in a dead-wall reverie. After a long silence: "Tell me a secret, Alex. What is grief?"

"After all those years, he hears your voice in the dark and goes straight for the shotgun. This is the definitive proof, Robert, because no man in the history of the world ever spontaneously tried to kill his adopted son. He was obviously your blood father."

Alex rises.

Back still to Alex: "A girl child, in a blue dress, about four or five months old. Like a doll."

Alex at refrigerator: "Murdered by the parents, who alone know the truth, and they're not going to confess forty-two years later, or maybe they're dead too. You want a little lunch? This crime is unsolvable. I'm making tuna sandwiches."

Robert turns at last, goes to table, requesting a sheet of paper and a pencil, which Alex promptly provides.

"I think I offered you a tuna sandwich."

Robert, sketching: "I have no appetite, except for tripe."

Alex, a man of his generation and circumstances: "What's tripe?"

"A metaphor for trash. Morris called it Italian chitlins."

"What are chitlins?"

"Morris loved both varieties. Intestines of pigs. Intestines of cows. Morris was surreptitiously broad-minded."

"Morris Reed was a secret multiculturalist of the bowels, who gave into pasta after you left. In loving memory of his dearly departed son."

"I would like to attempt a symbolic meal in honor of Morris Reed."

"They don't sell intestines anymore, not even in Utica. The Cornhill pyromaniacs prefer the Big Mac. The Italian-American assholes eat their veggie burgers in the suburbs."

"I never had the stomach for it. When Melvina put it on the table, I refused."

"Tripe or chitlins?"

"Both."

"Last night, when we got back, you looked green again. Food in general a problem for you?"

"I was never one for food, particularly after I left Utica. *[Pause.]* Last night I vomited again."

"Humans tend to eat."

"By the parents, or with the parents' knowledge and tacit consent, she was murdered."

"Did the Lebanese stickup artist have a child?"

"I don't know."

"When did the incident of Our Mother take place?"

"Winter of '54. So it is rumored among the sociologists of organized crime."

"It would explain the fate worse than death."

"Alex, this child was fair-complected. Her hair was light brown, verging on blond."

"Definitely not Lebanese. Forget about it, because even if at the time you had a camera, you realize how much they all look alike at that age? Assuming the same color? What are you drawing?"

"This, Alex, is your Tagliaferro guide to the past: a schematic rendering of the Spina backyard, circa 1954."

"This is the house, here's the garage. Obviously."

"And this little square here, a few feet behind the house, precisely here, almost on the eastern border of the lot, this little square represents the shed. And this big circle here, just north of the shed, this is the gigantic cherry tree, which is within the garden that runs all the way back here to the north end of the lot, alongside the garage. Like this. And this little circle next to the northeast corner of the garage, inside the garden, yes, precisely here, this is the fig tree."

"I never heard anyone talk like that, with all those compass directions."

"I was a keen sportsman, you recall. Then I lived on the grid of Manhattan, where they all talk that way. Pay attention. This very little circle inside the square of the shed, precisely at the mid-point of the square, at the intersection of the diagonals, this is where I buried her. Here she lies."

"You can't say the word precisely. This isn't an engineer's map."

"I can say it. Here she lies."

"The house and the garage remain. The rest is blacktop."

"The rest is silence."

"But so what, anyway? Even if assuming you're right about the location of what doesn't exist, so what? Okay. You could dig her up. You could walk to the exact spot with a pick and shovel and in no time you could find the skeleton. If you alert the police, guess what happens next? They think, Hey! He's the one. You buried her? Forty-two years ago? You must be the one overwhelmed by guilt at last. Take him downtown. They have no evidence, but you're in the news for weeks, under suspicion and ruined for the rest of your life."

"My life."

"They dig up the entire yard. They dig up the cellar. Because they believe you're a serial sex killer. They take one look at you and it's obvious you fit the profile to a 't.'"

"But I don't tell anyone that I buried her. I decide, after moving in, in a grand gesture of nostalgia, to return the backyard to its former condition. Utican remembers the way we were and does something about it. This is how they will print it. Makes sad discovery. Officials mystified. I accidentally find the skeleton in the excavation process."

"And this is how we destroy Spina. But the forensics point to death long before he laid down the blacktop. Plus where's the evidence to link him to the crime?"

"Nevertheless, the media feeds for weeks and this guarantees Spina's death as a politician."

"Which makes us both happy."

"We can't solve the crime, but we can put a muzzle on Muzzy. We can destroy the type of criminal who can't be incarcerated under the law."

"Then we're happy because we can say that this child died for a purpose revealed to us only now. In the fullness of time. God's in his heaven, all's right with the world."

"Alex, we've hit upon the solution of a very bad novelist. The plot drivers. Not even Dickens would try this. Should he learn that you were part of such a tawdry little shocker, Ayoub would be heartbroken. We of course abominate such thinking. I was kidding."

"Then this child died for no reason."

"Oh, somebody had a reason."

"This child's death brings no good to the future. No ironic reversals. No redemption."

"Perhaps it did the parents good at the time. It released some terrible tension in the marriage."

"Yeah, but then they couldn't sleep for the rest of their lives."

"Sentimental speculation from the tough guy. No, Alex, they lived happily ever after, raising many healthy children, because once the tension subsided they felt they were ready for children. This killing redeemed their marriage. It brought them happy children, who had happy children."

"You're worse than Ayoub."

"For me, this child's death will never be redeemed. [*Pause.*] On the other hand, Alex, bad novels have their uses. We could do it. A skeleton in his backyard! Three weeks from today, Spina's forever finished. The media loves nothing better than the bad novels of everyday life."

"So we do it."

"We don't do it."

"Then stop breaking my balls with this idea."

"If we do it, we reap but a short-term benefit. Spina himself is not the problem."

"Talk to me."

"We agree that we find this man offensive. You say that you hate him."

"I do surely hate him."

"Why? Can we put it into words? During my period at Proctor High, he too was a student there, and he was no different then. He disgusted me then. Why?"

"You want me to say that this is more than a personal repulsion. Our nausea goes beyond Spina, who symbolizes a political blah blah blah. Robert, it's going to be on the news tonight and in the paper tomorrow. He announced for mayor this morning on the steps of City Hall. For the occasion, his connection in the Department of Streets and Sewers brought the Pellettieri Ave sign, post and all, on a flat bed truck. At the end of his speech, Spina walks to the truck and points. He says, in this subtle combination Jewish and black undertone: 'Never again. We shall overcome.' He walks off giving the black power salute. He runs, he wins, unless he dies."

"At the final dinner, you will hear the end of the Utica story. Marchisi and the first Lucca. In order to honor them, we must dishonor what Spina stands for: blood pride. It's time for the Italian-Americans of Utica to pay this price, and Spina is the key. Let him win. Let him stand high in City Hall. Italian-American pride needs the forum and status of the mayoralty. A great victory comes before the fall."

"We are virtuous, because we are Italian."

"We will support and love each other, because we are Italian."

"It's a privilege to be a fucking Italian."

"I honor you, my Italian friend, though your values disgust me."

"The Italian-American people are a very great fucking people."

"The ascension of Spina will trigger epic Italian-American self-cleansing. They will loathe their ethnicity. They will all want to change their surnames to Windsor, Spencer, or Bowles."

"Once we strip away the film of white ethnic pride we find you, on Mary Street, the nigger lurking within. It's only a matter of time. Every month will be black heritage month, in which blacks learn of the honky in the woodpile, and vice versa."

"Yes yes! The dried up uterus revitalized in a post-ethnic and post-racial Utica. From the woodpile of impurity. In the beginning was impurity. We return to the beginning."

"Robert Tagliaferro returns to the scene of the crime to prophecy a general re-birth. A new world full of Robert Tagliaferros. *[Pause.]* This is only personal. This whole thing of yours."

"Gregorio Spina prophesied that I would commit murder."

"On the basis of your character, this can't be done. Gregorio Spina was a bad novelist."

"My life. My character. You claim to know what particular action may plausibly follow from it?"

"Not murder. I'll know it when I see it."

"Alex, my character is your forced fiction. I exist in the drifts of my own ashen artificialities, in a speech wrenched here and there, helter skelter, from the grounded worlds of great writers. Wrenched. Fantastic. We invent ourselves in order to become corpses. As Mr. Fitzgerald said, 'We leak sawdust.' "

Alex places a tuna sandwich and a glass of milk before Robert, saying, "Eat this, it absorbs the sawdust." Robert says, "The negative is still in force," and Alex says, "Good. I'll eat them both and drink this one too." When he's finished, he says: "Between the amounts you put in, which except for the first night are the amounts of a two-year-old, and what your body prematurely rejects, I can't figure out how you exist. The way you talk about food, you're a kid with his nose pressed against the window of the candy store. But then they let you in and say, Eat to your heart's content, kid, but for some reason you suddenly have no appetite."

"My life. My character. My heart's content."

"Who is Robert the Tagliaferro, that we should weep for him?"

"You yourself have a little ashen artificiality. The mark of Ayoub? Alex, Sebastian Spina will live and I will frustrate Gregorio Spina's pulp fiction destiny for me."

"How could anybody shape your destiny? You've got a head like a rock."

"In opera *buffa,* the villain does not die a physical death. Spina must live."

"They're on to you, Robert."

"The cherry tree was gigantic, Alex."

"They're on to you, Robert."

"Excuse me?"

"They all know you're not who you say you are. Mr. Forza."

"You're sure of this?"

"And guess what?"

"What?"

"They don't care that much, one way or the other."

Silence.

"They're not stunned, Robert. They're not intrigued, thrilled, or outraged."

"They don't care that much, one way or the other?"

"Once Paternostra and Hudson assured themselves that you're not a hit man, why should anyone care that much what name you use? Spina gets his money regardless. And what could it matter to Cesso or Ayoub? Who's living in a cheap novel now, Robert?"

"The cherry tree was gigantic."

"Okay. I take the bait."

"We'll save it for the last dinner."

"Cheap. *[Pause.]* I'm out of here."

"I would appreciate your company."

"I have to talk to Spina about the new closing date. Then I'm going to see Heather about an urn."

"Are you speaking in code?"

"What?"

"Urn or uterus?"

"Hey, Robert. Do me a favor."

"Certainly."

"Do the dishes."

Chapter 10

So he does the dishes, happily, because he has nothing else to do, and into the doing he disappears. Then too soon finished, and he's by himself, with nothing to do, except be himself. Who now is Robert?

He's read all the books, taken all the notes. Has no desire to walk the streets of the east side, and with Morris dead feels no reason to. Tolerates food, just barely. In ten days, he'll move to the two-family house where Spina has lived alone for years. Spina will empty the house of all furniture, then leave. Then Robert will move in with his four suitcases. Then what? Wait for Alex's monthly visits? There will be one more dinner, just one more, at which he'll finish the story. What shall he do in the interim, before the move to 1303 Mary Street? Assuming that he finds something to occupy himself for the interim (but what could it possibly be?), what does he do after the move? For forty-two years, he had prepared himself so thoroughly, to do what takes but a few hours: tell the stories around the dinner table, as he, by virtue of his telling, commits assault and battery. Gives no thought about what he's also been doing since his return. The various acts of charity: of this doing on behalf of Alex Lucas he is thoughtless, perhaps, because this doing is not propelled by forethought. Unlike his storytelling, his charity is a sudden springing up in the moment. Once done, he reflects not at all upon what he has done and is conscious only of a pleasant feeling in the moment of the doing, and a little afterwards. If asked, But why Alex? He would not have been able to give a cogent response. He would not have said, Why *not* Alex? Because he was not thoughtless in that sense. Surely there was something deeper, far down. The pleasant feeling, if interrogated, or the act of charity beneath it, and what was beneath the act, *that* might have told him what was there, far down, had he looked beneath, which he did not, because about this feeling, about this act of charity, and whatever lay beneath, all the way down, about that he was not inquisitive and would not become upset if told that beneath his eruptions into charity lay nothing at all.

This is what he knows in Alex's kitchen: that he wants to stay there, rather than go below to his room. He sits in Alex's kitchen, thinking that he and Alex and Spina lived alone. Ayoub had a live-in girlfriend but, in truth, lived intimately only with his thoughts and books and scribblings. Like himself. What he'd learned about the lives of writers was that when the work goes well they have bounce in their voices, actually seem to be conscious of you, and show a little kindness. When it's going badly, they're monsters of walking death. Paternostra and Hudson, he suspected, had a marriage with the usual highs and lows, but mostly it was a good marriage, a broad sustaining river, a flow not dramatically evident to the eye, of low key and uneventful mutuality. The friendship of Paternostra and Cesso? A dark secret? Nonsense. Domestic birds of a feather, that's all, spending much time in kitchens, helping to put away the groceries, conversing at meals. Cesso lived within an easy walk of Paternostra and never called before-hand. I thought I'd just drop in, Joseph, and say hello, bearing a bag of freshly picked tomatoes from his garden. In his politics, even Spina had found comity of sorts, and soon Alex and Heather, and so forth, and Ayoub, after all, still had his books and scribblings, and until he used up all the books, and finished writing his book about hell, and could scribble no more, he wouldn't need to deal with the horror of himself. Alex's theory about Morris had not unveiled himself to himself, his own horror had not jumped up, perhaps because he'd already entertained such a theory, not to explain his paternity, but in one elegant insight to grasp the fate worse than death of the Lebanese stickup artist and Paternostra's indulgence of Ayoub's relentless nastiness. Ayoub? The son of the Lebanese stickup artist, torn from his mother's breast, given to Abraham Ayoub, and the stickup artist told: you must never speak to your son, or he dies. He, not you. Never speak. Never touch. No contact. You must acknowledge his presence in no way when you pass on the street. Not even a nod of civility. A year later, the crook-father did himself the favor of blowing his own brains out. Which was a fact. The only fact. The rest is a popular novel. A story that Ayoub need not, and would not hear, not from him. Just as Heather would not learn, not from him, the story of Theodore Faxton, who started in old Utica as a stagecoach driver and ended with a hospital named after him, all of the beds of which might have been occupied by those whom old Theodore had . . . and so on. Heather surely had heard. But Heather Faxton is a Faxton in name only, who does not inherit the sins of her fathers. He'll spare her. Nothing in a name.

Looks down at his historical rendering of 1303 Mary Street. He's like a visitor to Rome who sees neither the contemporary city all before him, nor the ruins of the ancient city, but the ancient city itself as it actually was in its various phases. Not serially, but as if they were co-present and graspable in a single glance. The city of Aurelian, surrounded by walls. And before that, the Rome of the republic and early Caesars. And before that, the phase of the Septimontium, the first federation of settlements on the seven hills. And before that, oldest Rome: the *Roma Quadrata,* the first fenced settlement on the Palatine. Just so this man of books and notes sees old Utica. Having glimpsed it, will no longer see, wills himself not to see, contemporary Utica. Where his physical self is, Robert Tagliaferro almost is not. He clings to the present, no longer knowing why he clings, only that he clings, and that it is very difficult to cling. He's thinking about it. That he'd prefer to let go.

He says, aloud, smiling a little, "Curiosity killed the cat, but for a while it will keep me from letting go." What, exactly, he wonders, is a pulverizer, and could one be rented on an hourly basis? Alex was the last Lucas in Utica, but where were his parents, who were likely still alive, and, if so, why hadn't Alex yet mentioned them? What would become of his two-year-old daughter? Would she live with her father again, who would certainly, before the year was out, be living with Heather? If Alex's theory of his paternity is valid, then who decided on Tagliaferro for his surname? Morris? The putative Italian-American mother? Why Tagliaferro? In the few hours he'd spent with Morris upon his return, he was surprised by Morris's sense of humor. He remembered no such thing from his youth: no humor with an acerbic edge and the hint of a knowledgeable reserve. Had he not died, Robert was ready to spring his pet historical notion about the name. Just to gauge the reaction. Robert believed that the name had its origin in the sophisticated civilization on the Italian peninsula that had antedated the Romans, the first great Italian culture, 1000 B.C., economically founded in the Colline Metallifere, those metal-bearing hills above the major cities of the Etruscans. Among ancient cultures of the West, the most mysterious. Did Morris somehow know of the Etruscans? Of the rich yield of iron, copper, and silver that became the basis of their economy? The Etruscan iron, fashioned into fearful weaponry. The engine of Etruscan society and power was the iron cutter, *il tagliaferro,* most honored craftsman of the Iron Age. The craftsman? Or the chisel with which he performed his work? I am Robert the Chisel. His surname was Morris's joke and pride. In order to say that I, me, Morris Reed, a nigger: from my loins into the very soul of Italy. My son, the essential Italian. Ha. "Mr. Eliot saith," saith Robert aloud, "a perpetual possibility, only in a world of speculation." Mr. Reed is dead. Mr. Eliot too. Ha. The Etruscan language, Robert had read, of which we know almost nothing, has no kin among the known tongues. The writer had put it that way: no kin. The Etruscans were indigenous to the Italian pen-insula as Robert believed that he, himself, was indigenous to Utica: in a virtual sort of way. He wondered about the Etruscan word for *il tagliaferro.* Did they invent it? Take it? Was there one?

What becomes of a storyteller when not telling stories?

———➤◆◄———

Alex returns at the dinner hour, carrying a large box, to find Robert sitting at the kitchen table, eating a sandwich. Half sand-wich in hand. On the small plate before him, the other half. A glass of milk. Plate and milk on a place mat. Place mat is the sketch of 1303 Mary Street. "Eating" is too strong.

As Alex enters, Robert says, "What is a pulverizer, and can one rent a nonindustrial model on an hourly basis?"

Alex replies, "I finally figured it out. It's me, not you, who's lost his mind. You couldn't wait for me to come home? You're spoiling your appetite."

"Are you insulted? This is the leftover tuna. I'm making an effort. What's in the box? A surprise for me?"

"Something from Heather for you. I told her your whole story, including the part about Sir Thomas. In this box is her reaction."

"Show me."

"Anticipation and delay are good."

"A mini-pulverizer?"

"A pulverizer is a machine for smashing things down. I saw a movie where they reduced an entire car with a person in it to the size of your fist. Food substances can be reduced to powder form."

"A skeleton can be reduced to the appearance of crushed sea shells."

"Crown Hill has its own pulverizer. Industrial strength."

"Show me what's in the box."

"No."

"Please."

"Later."

"Alex, you've become a pulp novelist. Here's more grist for your mill. I require a pulverizer for the blue doll. Her delicate skeleton will easily be processed by a nonindustrial model. Then I can mix her with Morris, in kinship of skeletal fragments. A childless father and a parentless daughter, together at last. That would close the book, I think."

"You intend to dig her up after all?"

"Intend is too strong."

"Are you, or aren't you?"

"Just a thought. *[Pause.]* Show me what's in there."

"No."

"I'm ready for the final dinner, which we will resist calling The Last Supper. Please make the arrangements for tomorrow evening. Between now and then I will sleep. Until eight, tomorrow evening, I will not leave my bed. Tomorrow is July the seventh, the sixth day of my return. And on the seventh day I shall rest. How long do you intend to stand there holding that box?"

Alex puts box down. Sits. Takes untouched half sandwich and eats it, saying: "You're not going to eat this anyway." Finishes, saying: "Spina starts to balk a little when I tell him ten days, so I say: 'Mr. Forza can take his seventy large elsewhere, because I happen to know that one block east from here a house is going on the market soon.' Naturally, I'm lying. He says, 'Don't get me wrong. I was just talking.' I say, 'I didn't get you wrong, sir. You don't have a skeleton in your closet, do you? Because it should be revealed before the final papers are signed.' He turns red. I decide to go all out to break his balls. I say, 'Alderman Spina, there's nothing to the rumor that there's a body under your blacktop?' He turns purple, like the raw ass of one of those monkeys. I say, 'I was just kidding, sir.' I put my arm around his shoulders and say, 'But I wouldn't want to be the one who broke the color barrier on this block, just between us.' He explodes. He says, 'Don't tell me you and Forza are fronting a coon!' So I say, 'Sir, in all honesty, do I look like a nigger-lover?' When I say that, it's like he's injected with a massive tranquilizer. *[Pause.]* Ten days from now, we're ready to rock, splish splash I was taking a bath!"

"Spina is hiding something damaging to his reputation, but we don't care."

"Then I pay a visit to Darryl."

"Darryl Crouse?"

"To tell him that the ashes aren't coming to him directly, but not to worry, in the end he'll be pleased with the mode of presentation."

"You used that phrase?"

"He asks me what I mean by that phrase and I tell him all about Heather's gift."

"The surprise which I can now easily imagine. You gave away too much too early."

"Darryl's ruined. He looked like he'd been crying for a week."

"Inconsolable."

"That's the word."

"Good."

"Good?"

"As you were upon Caroline's death. It's the right thing. Darryl is real."

"How long do you intend to keep the ashes?"

"Not long."

"Then I went to Heather."

"You promised Darryl before you went to Heather?"

"I know Heather."

"How much time did you spend with Spina?"

"About twenty minutes."

"And with Darryl?"

"About forty minutes."

"This would take us to about 1:00 P.M. It's now almost six. The discussion with Heather about my past, and about classical cinerary urns, must have been extensively detailed, Alex."

"We talked maybe an hour."

"This would take us to about 2:00 P.M. Where did you go for the next four hours?"

"I stayed there."

"For extensive personal conversation."

"Is that supposed to be code, circa 1954?"

Robert blushes. Says, "I was speaking literally, Alex. Not making an intimate allusion."

"We talked a little. In between."

Alex blushes.

"What will you do about your daughter?"

Across Alex's face, a flash of anger. Then a blankness.

"Nothing."

"You don't want her to be with you in your new life?"

"In the first year, my parents came up from Florida to help. They lived downstairs for a year. She must have sensed that my mother was her mother. I'm sure of it. My mother was her mother. As much as I could, I was involved. Eventually, it wasn't right. I sent them back to their retired life, even though they were willing to move back permanently. Willing and even happy. I moved her to New York, to Caroline's sister and brother-in-law. A couple in their forties with two kids in college. I broke the

bond she had with me and my parents. I destroyed it. That was
bad for her. Very bad. I won't tell you the details. Now she's
bonded and secure again, with my in-laws. Except for the blood,
she's their daughter. You think I'm going to break another bond
at this age? She can't lose her third mother and second father at
the age of two. It'll never happen. It would be a vicious crime.
I suggested that they adopt her, and they agreed. I'll see her when
I can, as much as I can."

"And you'll make a new life with Heather."

"That's your dream, for some reason."

"You lost your wife. And your daughter."

"I won't tear her out of her home just because I'm the father.
My fatherhood is not quite empty, but soon, in a few years, it will
be. Absolutely empty. What else is there to say?"

"Nothing."

The clock says 6:45.

Alex says, "I'm going to bed." Drinks Robert's untouched
glass of milk. Says, "I'd better make the arrangements for tomorrow night." Looks at phone on wall. Does not rise.

"And then show me what's in the box?"

Silence.

"Alex?"

"What?"

"The box?"

"What about it?"

"Will you show me the surprise now?"

Alex leans over and pulls it from the box, sets it upon the
table. About two feet in height with handles.

Robert says, "Exactly as described by Sir Thomas Browne.
Except for the handles, the classic shape of the cinerary urn–
uterus. But it looks new."

"Heather says this is an exceptional nineteenth-century forgery,
which she bought from a private party in Athens. Based on a
ninth-century B.C. original. After I gave her your deep background,

after I told her your current needs, she says, 'This is the one, but tell him it's not called a cinerary urn, though it may be used as such.' She's giving it to you. It's a storage vase, that's why they put handles on. Typically for wine. I'm going to bed now. I have to. They also used these things as grave markers. Heather says that there was a time in the early part of this century when pottery craftsmen in Athens produced imitations of the ancient ash urns, but nobody bought them. They used this particular vase in its time to mark women's graves."

"What does this lone figure here signify? It appears to be a hooded youth."

"She says the scholars can't agree. In her reading in the field, she could never learn why they favored this one for women. The historians had nothing to say about the question. They call it a belly-handled vase, which she says gave her a thought. Heather says it should be called a pregnant-belly vase. Look, Robert: this is the shape of the third trimester. She says the key is the wavy line encircling the vase precisely at the bulge. It accentuates the bulge. According to Heather, it's an homage to the female. The pagan veneration of the fertile woman. Now look at this. *[Goes back into box. Removes a book. Opens to an illustration.]* It's obvious. This is her point. This is a relief sculptured about 25,000 B.C. What can such a date mean? These people were lean. They were hard. They worked out seven days a week. Look at this. The breasts so heavy with milk."

"Veritable udders."

"Look at this belly. These thighs! The overall girth of the mid-body. She says this type of thing is found from Siberia to France, 25,000 B.C. The hand caresses the bulge. She feels the kick within. She's soothing the child inside her. Heather says that the historians speak stupidly about it. They refer to the first examples of an artistic genre. The female nude. They use the word Venus."

"The soothing is a promise to the child within, the child conceived with anticipatory images of what must befall it when it tumbles forth. What is this writing below the wavy line? What does it mean?"

"The scholars say this combination of letters is totally meaningless. Heather is saying this is the first Madonna and Child, and this belly vase is a reference to an obsessive image. The deepest human representation of nature is the Madonna and Child. According to Heather. The relief and the vase are references to nature. So I ask her if that's nature, where is the male in nature? She answers that she's willing to bet that the man who reads Sir Thomas Browne knows the answer to my question. I say, 'What are you willing to bet?' She says, 'If he doesn't give you the correct answer, he doesn't get the vase.' Then I say, 'If he does?' She laughs and says, 'You'll see.' I say, 'How will I know if it's right unless I check with you?' She says, 'You won't need to check, if it's right.' So what's your answer, Robert?"

"25,000 B.C. The primal sculptor. He who needs to venerate in mimetic homage the one incontrovertible creative principle. It's the origin of art. The male who needs."

"This has been said before."

"Yes. For 25,000 years. The male emerges from the mother, then spends the remainder of his life trying to represent the mother. A mama's boy. A sissy. *In utero,* forget genital difference. *In utero,* total femaleness. On this earth, when at last a male, he walks but briefly, to and fro, in terrible independence: a deviation from nature. Don't fuck with me! I am a man! In death, after death, only the female. Back inside her oblivion. Secured forever from tumbling forth. Promise redeemed. Nature. God."

"I don't think I need to check with Heather."

"The belly vase."

"The belly vase."

Alex rises. Makes call. Says, "I'm going to bed." Leaves.

Robert at table. Folding and unfolding the sketch of 1303 Mary Street. Folding and unfolding.

The Final Dinner

Eleven A.M. Alex bears Morris's ashes away, as Robert wakes, lightened and happy in the first instant of consciousness. He wants, of all things, mercy to be the legacy of his storytelling.

Alex does not hesitate. Goes directly to Robert's shade-drawn room, carrying a small covered plastic bucket, pink, a child's sandbox toy, labeled: Courtesy of Crown Hill Memorial Park.

Robert says, "A good person, upon whom everything depended, suddenly no longer exists. Caroline Lucas the first. Now Heather is here and you've landed, after much turbulence, on your feet. Despair vanquished. Anger routed. Happy days are here again."

"Correct. Except you forget one thing. You of all people."

"What's that, Alex?"

"My memory."

"We're moving on."

"We or me?"

"We. We're moving on."

"The good person who suddenly no longer exists, who we need. I thought you were referring to Morris Reed."

"Rhyme. The cognitive power of a witty rhyme."

"I didn't intend it."

"Splendid!"

Silence.

"I was surprised by the smallness of this thing."

"Morris Reed withered into the truth."

"This isn't even half full."

"You looked inside?"

"But it's a lot heavier than it looks. Are you actually going to stay in bed all day until the dinner?"

"So much the better to compose my thoughts, for the last act. In this semi-dark. [Pause.] I need to look inside that thing."

Robert sits up. Alex brings bucket. Robert requests a teaspoon and a letter-sized envelope. Alex complies. Robert opens bucket. Stares for many seconds. Then spoons, once, but heapingly, into the envelope: "The rest is Darryl's. Feel free to deliver it to him, at your convenience, in the belly vase. Please don't mention that what you bring is not quite complete."

"Need anything before I go?"

"No."

"My refrigerator is yours."

"Thank you."

"After Darryl, I've got paper work at the bank and the lawyer's on the Spina property. I'll be back just before eight."

"I need something."

"What?"

"A lachrymatory."

"A what?"

"After the bank and the lawyer's, and before eight, during those several hours that you'll be spending with her, in one of those rare moments of speaking, ask. She knows."

Alex removes pen from his shirt pocket, a piece of paper from his wallet. Walks to wall, for a hard writing surface. Says: "Spell it."

⟫・0・⟪

They approach the trap door at Joe's, and it's apparent. They descend, and it's obvious. The absence of aroma from Raymond's *capretto alla romana,* slowly in the ovens grilling to the state of succulence. Alex, who lives now on another plane, is not fazed. Robert is the disappointed child of Christmas morning. The men stand to greet them. On one side wall, an Italian flag has been pinned. On the other, an American flag.

Ayoub says, gesturing to the flags, "Alderman Spina's decorations. His counterstatement."

Spina says, "In answer to Mr. Forza's insinuendos against America and her Italian people, who are her greatest people."

Raymond, pointing to Robert: "Look at this poor bastard! Mr. Forza, I got here at five to fire up and when nothing happens

I go crazy, because I know you need *capretto* like some people need a piece of ass. When we get the call that the dinner is off, I had five nice ones marinating for almost two days in lemon and olive oil. The recipe calls for a day and a half. What could I do? I rape the recipe. I keep marinating in the fond hopes that somebody changes his mind. Again the phone. It's on for tonight. Three days in the lemon and olive oil. It's ready to fall off the bone and melt in my mouth, so who needs to cook it? Slurp and swallow! Did I mention the levels of garlic, pepper, and rosemary? Don't force me to disclose the salt, because somebody is going to break my balls again anyway about the salt, this is what he does. Raymond, you put too much salt. Raymond, you forgot to put salt. I hate the word salt. The pressure I face day in and day out in my own home concerning condiments is tremendous. *[Pause.]* Mildly gamy-tasting. Medium rare. Hot on the tongue. Then the ovens, so help me God, you tell me, okay? You tell me where I'm going to get somebody who does this kind of work to come over here at five o'clock on a Sunday night."

"Raymond, it's Friday."

"So what? *[Pause.]* So what? The faint scent of wild thyme. Mr. Forza, do you follow? Why don't I hear suggestions from the floor? Two tablespoons of ground ginger. The broccoli. The rice. Right down the toilet. You know what you're going to get instead, Mr. Forza? *[Pause.]* Tell me, why am I asking you? Why? Because how the fuck would you know? Remember what you had plastered all over your dome the other night? The color of that is my clue to you, which it's obvious rings no bells. Green! Pesto! Pasta in a pesto sauce, which is being made upstairs by John personally. Which reminds me where I'm needed." Raymond ascends. He's gone.

Ayoub says, "No kid for you, Mr. Forza."

They settle into their respective chairs. Paternostra pours the wine. A touch of gloom in the room, except for Alex, who glows, and in the glowing gathers the gloom about him. Paternostra gazes up to the trap door and says, "He's sensitive. Of course, Raymond overstates the domestic tension, which is normal."

Cesso, with full understanding of what he's saying: "Like my wife. Raymond reminds me of her." Cesso's boldness silences Spina, who appears to strangle a little on what there is no longer to say, because it has been said.

Alex says, "I'll eat anything."

Robert smiles.

Paternostra turns to Alex and says, "Yes."

Spina: "Mr. Forza obviously won't start in until after we eat. So how about it, Professor? Tell us about this so-called book of yours you're supposedly writing for how many years? Help us to kill a little time before the main event, which is how I phrase it, Professor, knowing you'll vote even for one of that element, rather than for me. Think I don't know? In which case I too can take off the gloves in this cellar of ours. In other words, Professor, go fuck yourself."

Silence. Ayoub, in the silence, grinning.

Paternostra: "Now you have broken the rules."

Cesso: "He ripped the fabric of our thing."

Paternostra: "He put himself outside."

Alex (cheerfully): "This is irretrievable."

Paternostra: "Now you destroy yourself."

Spina: "Why should I be singled out? When I consider the amount of insinuation that goes on in this place, why me? Because I'm a plain-spoken American? He's going to vote for the nigger. Everyone knows this. For this, my honesty, I have to suffer?"

Paternostra: "Yes."

Cesso: "You must suffer."

Spina: "Why?"

Paternostra: "The type of comment you made doesn't nurture the conversation. It clogs. And then where are we?"

Alex: "You stopped the show, sir."

Spina: "I sincerely doubt it."

Ayoub: "There is a basis for your doubt, Sebastian. Never doubt that. I'm grateful to Sebastian. 'Go fuck yourself.' The title of chapter eight of *The Music of the Inferno.* 'Go fuck yourself.' The key to my meditative variations on Milton's account of the origin of sin and death in the second book of *Paradise Lost.*"

Spina: "Who's the Jew?"

Ayoub: "Sebastian?"

Spina: "Who's this Jew, Milton? This writer, this Jew."

Alex: "He was a Christian."

Spina: "He was a writer."

Robert: "You are not totally wrong."

Ayoub: "He's totally right. I, myself, am a kind of Jew."

Spina: "You said it. I'm not a writer, let's be clear about that."

Ayoub: " 'Go fuck yourself.' Satan heard those words in heaven, when all was well, and those words were coterminous with his rebellion against the Father and the terrible diminishment of this, the brightest of angels. 'Go fuck yourself.' The entire narrative follows from that. 'Go fuck yourself.' "

Spina: "You found your level, Professor. Don't tell me I'm wrong, Albert, because you know I'm right."

Cesso: "You're not wrong, Sebastian. Louis's way is the negative way."

Paternostra: "Once more into the mire, dear friends."

Cesso: "It's traditional among the Desert Fathers."

Ayoub: "The condition of heaven and the condition of earth is the condition of freedom. God respects his creation. He creates by withdrawing Himself, and man, like the angels, is free, thanks to His generosity. Free to connect or to disconnect. To hook up or to say no. Before Satan's rebellion, there was no disconnection. The angels chose to connect, to serve the Father, and in serving Him they acquired the strength and peace of connected being."

Paternostra: "Who spoke that awful language to Satan?"

Ayoub: "Nobody."

Robert: "The Arch Fiend spoke those words to himself. When he contemplated himself as a separate being, he became a separate being. He cut himself off. He looked at himself, as if in a mirror. I am me. I am the Father, the Mother, and Me. I need nobody. I am me me me. The entire narrative follows."

Paternostra: "He put himself outside."

Cesso: "Like Sebastian."

Paternostra: "In here, we've got each other, and ourselves."

Cesso: "Outside, Sebastian's got himself."

Paternostra: "Outside, Sebastian's got nothing."

Spina: "That's too extreme, Joseph."

Cesso: "You're very human, Sebastian. Like my children, when one of them is naughty, we say 'you have to go to the time-out chair.' Where they must sit alone, outside the family circle. Like little devils. They cry until we let them back in."

Robert: "The fiends below can't ever get back in. How they cry!"

Cesso: "Why should they get back in after what they did?"

Paternostra: "No mercy can be shown. In other words, don't blame me when I come down on the back of your head. Don't beg me when I have to do what you in so many words asked for."

Ayoub: "You, Joseph? The back of the head?"

Paternostra: "I was referring to the Father, who we have a tendency to identify with. The wrath, I'm referring to. The wrath is not a personal issue."

Alex: "Satan looked at himself and said, 'You're beautiful.'"

Ayoub: "Which is coterminous with?"

Alex: " 'Go fuck yourself.' "

Ayoub: "Correct."

Alex: "Because who needs any body? If I can fuck myself."

Spina: "You say to me, Joseph, I broke the rules? Me? And you listen to this pornography, and you have nothing to say? You're breaking my heart, Joseph."

Paternostra: "At this moment, Sebastian, I would leave, if I didn't sense something underneath."

Spina: "A deeper sewer."

Cesso: "Maybe the opposite of the sewer, Sebastian."

Paternostra: "A fragrance."

Robert: "The condition of hell is also the condition of earth. As Mr. Milton knew. Willful and bitter severance. *Non serviam*. I am me."

Alex: "You look in the mirror."

Robert: "And you say, to quote Raymond, Who, pray tell, who the fuck are you, in truth?"

Ayoub: "Maybe the scapegoat. Mr. Forza."

Paternostra: "You are not Mr. Forza, Mr. Forza. This we know. It matters not to us who you really are. Nevertheless: Who are you, Mr. Forza?"

Cesso: "Who are you, Mr. Forza?"

Robert: "I am an exceptional nineteenth-century forgery."

Paternostra: "Good."

Cesso: "Good."

Spina: "You know what this is all about? This is about breaking my balls something terrific."

Paternostra: "Who are you, Mr. Forza?"

Robert: "I am Tagliaferro! The walking encyclopedia of Utica, New York."

Spina to Alex: "Remember: I keep the five hundred, regardless."

Cesso: "This is your name? Robert Tagliaferro?"

Robert: "Yes."

Spina to Alex: "So far I signed nothing binding. Don't forget."

Paternostra: "Who are you, Mr. Tagliaferro?"

Robert: "I am no one."

Ayoub: "Odysseus, quote unquote."

Robert: "I am one sorry devil."

Spina: "Heh, heh. Nothing binding, Alex."

Alex to Spina: "He's as good as gold."

Ayoub: "He said to himself, Go fuck yourself. The statement was coterminous with the act."

Cesso: "So to speak, Louis. Surely."

Ayoub: "No. He truly fucked himself."

Spina: "And this is the fragrance under the sewer."

Paternostra: "This is written down!? This Milton actually wrote this down on paper?"

Ayoub: "In effect."

Cesso: "In other words, so to speak, Louis."

Spina: "He made the filth up. The Professor."

Ayoub: "Then he gave birth."

Robert: "He had a baby."

Paternostra: "Who?"

Alex: "Satan."

Paternostra: "This should not be mentioned to Raymond. Ever."

Cesso: "So to speak, Louis."

Ayoub: "No. Milton put it in writing. It was a girl."

Robert: "The child he would not recognize."

Ayoub: "He, Satan, looked in the mirror and was perplexed. And she said—"

Alex: "The mirror said."

Ayoub: "Yes. The mirror, the girl child said:

> 'Likest to thee in shape and count'nance bright,
> Then shining heav'nly fair, a Goddess admir'd
> Out of thy head I sprung . . .'

In the isolated pleasure of self-incest, from the vagina of the mind, she springs."

Alex: "The original mind-fuck and its issue."

Robert: "Coterminous and co-present: self-consciousness, the directive to fornicate oneself, the very act, and its foul issue. Call it the metaphysics of Evil, which is disconnection. Call it Satan's fantasia of pure independence."

Ayoub: "She was called Sin."

Spina: "Filth and big words. Have you ever taught in a college, Mr. Tagliaferro?"

Robert: "Professor Ayoub, the antidote to the infernal vision lies in the work of a very great prose poet of your acquaintance. A great son of Utica."

Ayoub: "Gene?"

Alex: "Professor Nassar!"

Robert: "Yes, Mr. Nassar has fought this evil with longing, lyrical words."

Robert removes a slip of paper, much-crumpled and yellowed, and reads: " 'And he was his father (he hoped), otherwise, he was only himself, and that was not enough.' From Mr. Nassar's early work, *East Utica,* page 70. Look it up! It's in the book!"

Alex: "Unless our fathers are included in ourselves, we're satanic. We're selfish self-fuckers."

Robert: "Mr. Nassar's words are precise, Alex. He writes: 'not enough.' We are incomplete. And this is the state of damnation. In hell, irredeemable. Here, maybe we have a chance."

Ayoub: "I am that father whom your boyhood lacked, and suffered pain for lack of. I am he. Quote unquote. Not from a piece of paper, but from here. Lodged in here."

Ayoub is pointing to his head.

Spina: "The cunt of your mind?"

Robert: "Once, in similar circumstances, when I made a similar gesture, I was told it was my ass."

Cesso: "Such words that the Professor quoted are what Our Father in heaven will say to us, God willing."

Paternostra: "Were you quoting the Bible, Professor?"

Ayoub: "Homer. The long-lost Odysseus, speaking to his unhappy son. *[Pause.]* Milton is relentless. The idea of how Sin originated gave him the idea for the origin of Death. The wages of incest is incest."

Spina: "He banged his own daughter?"

Alex: "Who was, in a sense, himself."

Robert: "It could not be otherwise. The wages of disconnection is deeper disconnection."

Ayoub: "Sin, who is the mirror, tells her father *[again from memory, smiling, pointing to his head]:*

> Thyself in me thy perfect image viewing
> Becam'st enamor'd, and such joy thou took'st
> With me in secret, that my womb conceiv'd
> A growing burden . . . till my womb
> Pregnant by thee, and now excessive grown
> Prodigious motion felt and rueful throes.
> At last this odious offspring . . .
> Thine own begotten, breaking violent way
> Tore through my entrails . . .

And Son of Satan is born, whom she named Death, and whom she fled. And he, Death, pursued her in lust."

Spina: "First the father, before he's the father, bangs himself, and gives birth to the daughter, who he then bangs, the daughter, who gives birth to the son, who he, the son, now is also banging, the daughter, who is also the mother, who is also obviously the father, is what you're saying this fucking Milton is saying."

Ayoub: " 'A' plus, Sebastian. There is more to the mystery of the Infernal Trinity."

Robert: "The Infernal Trinity is not satiated. Therein lies its infernality. More self-fornication is on the way."

Ayoub: "Death, the son, rapes Sin, in embraces forcible and foul, and she begets monstrous dogs, who are 'hourly conceiv'd' and 'hourly born.' There is more. Listen. These dogs constantly return to the womb, up her vagina, howling and gnawing on her bowels, their repast. In and out, constantly eating her innards for dinner."

Robert: "We disconnect in order to eat ourselves alive. Satan, Sin, Death, and the Dogs who are forever famished. Coterminous and co-present. The hunger that cannot be satisfied. The hunger to be Me, Me! Nothing is enough. The howling of the dogs, Professor, is it, perchance, what you mean by the music of the inferno?"

Ayoub: "Several pages of an endless score."

Alex: "Why not Prof? Why not print *The Music of the Inferno* in a single volume with Professor Nassar's *East Utica*?"

Ayoub stares at Alex.

Alex: "His paradiso with your inferno."

Robert: "The full, the connected vision."

Ayoub stares at Robert. Grins. Points to his head. Says: "I've been writing this book for seventeen years. Myself am hell. Go fuck yourself."

Cesso: "Those dogs running in and out of the womb. Something occurs to me. May we not in this way imagine what these mothers suffer who abort? The baby who is not there, yet in a way still there, inside her, in her mind, gnawing, as you say, Louis. An eternal gnawing. The hunger that cannot be satisfied. Am I wrong?"

Ayoub: "This is not Milton, Albert. This is you."

Spina: "Amen."

Cesso: "Yes. This is me. But am I wrong? About those mothers and how they suffer?"

Paternostra: "Tell me one thing, Professor, and make me a happy man. Why must such an idea, which is a deep idea, maybe the deepest, which I call loyalty, why must this idea be said in such filthy words?"

Ayoub: "Because of all things filthy, Joseph, intentional disconnection is the filthiest. No worse there is none. I am the scholar of filth."

Robert: "In hell, there is much deluded self-knowledge."

Raymond, descending, with a large bowl under his arm, saying: "Did I miss much? Don't tell me."

Spina: "I'll give you one clue. Don't ever again say the words, 'Go fuck yourself.'"

Raymond: "In this cellar, the beauty of this cellar is that we don't have to be dishonest with each other. *[Places bowl of pasta on table.]* Every man's dream is that he could do those words. John won't help me bring it down. Who needs his help, I tell him? I have to make two more trips."

Alex: "I'll give you a hand."

"I don't accept."

———➤•◀———

For seven men, John has prepared three pounds of linguine, because it is his belief that a grown man eats almost a half pound at a sitting. A pesto sauce is rich and heavy. To eat almost a half pound of linguine in such a sauce is (in effect) to eat the equivalent of three quarters of a pound of linguine. Plenty of Italian bread, and a salad of arugola and endive, whose size is predicted by John's belief about a grown man's capacity for pasta. Robert eats almost nothing. Cesso, Paternostra, and Spina eat portions whose modesty radically belie John's belief. Alex eats according to John, and Raymond and Ayoub, in satanic character, consume the rest.

No single theme embraces the conversation. Anticipation of what Ayoub calls "the concluding chapter" is only enhanced by Robert's almost silent presence. Perhaps it is just that, Robert's almost silence, that spurs each of the men to his most provocative effort to fill the void.

Ayoub announces that his surname is Arabic for Job. No response. He says, "Believe me." No one looks up from his plate. Alex offers a mathematical fact that is taken for a real estate judgment. He says that 1303 Mary is prime. Spina grunts. Alex says, "1303 is indivisible, except by itself and the number one, which as divisors are trivial. It's prime. It's a rock." Spina inquires as to the effect on selling price. Then worries aloud about this meal's impact on his cholesterol. His enunciation of the key word sounds like "clustered hole." Raymond tells him that he knows a sure cure. But forget it, because you'll never find a human to give it to you. Then Paternostra describes the Mary of 1311 Mary Street. A bathtub of the free-standing type in the front yard, about a third of it sunken at one end in concrete. Feet sawed off, encircled by flowers, all set inside a square of bricks. Facing the street. The tub is a niche. Inside, a statue of the Virgin. He says, "I suppose eventually someone on Mary will get the thought to put in astroturf in the front yard." Robert looks at Alex. Alex blushes and says, "Poetic license." Cesso, in an attempt to create continuity, tells of what he's recently read about the Rome *Pièta*. How, if you examine the proportions, you see that Michelangelo made Christ with the body of a smallish twelve-year-old boy. Mary is twice his size. Maybe more. A boy in his mother's lap. According to Cesso, Michelangelo is "telling us something we should have guessed about Our Lord." Robert and Alex nod. Alex, trying to draw out Robert before the main event, says: "Tell us now the story about Gregorio Spina's gigantic cherry tree." Spina glances hostilely at Robert. Alex says, "As a warm-up." Robert says, "Not all the stories should be told." Paternostra asks Alex about "your young lady, who was supposed to join us for dinner. Did she decide against setting a precedent?" Alex replies, "She said that she might be quite late. That she would for sure join us for coffee." Raymond says, "There will be no coffee." Alex, after a long pause, looks at Robert and says, "Please." Robert says, "No."

Alex suggests that "Utica in itself, as we know it, and as an idea, the overwhelming idea of Utica," ought to be the subject of the last chapter of *The Music of the Inferno*. Ayoub says, "How did you guess?" Then Robert:

"And this, always, has been a place of fires."

"That sounds like something."

"Another forgery?"

"Yes," Robert says, "very late nineteenth century, 'And this too has been a place of darkness.' Mr. Conrad's sound and rhythm are superior. *[Pause.]* Somewhat. *[Pause.]* We acknowledge the fathers and suddenly we feel less visible. Less driven by the vicious thoughts of freedom and originality. Less responsible. Like children. *[Pause.]* Suddenly one feels better. In a way. I have many literary fathers. *[Pause.]* The fires of the nineties. Those of 1947 and '48. All preceded by the terrible rash of 1850 and '51. Ours consume houses, not businesses, and we suspect slumlords, insurance hungry, and the self-destruction of underclass blacks, who burn their own places, where they do not feel in place, as they burn with hunger for homes. With one exception, an accident perhaps, those of the late forties consumed only businesses, and we concur with contemporary observers that an obscure anarchist was likely at work. But the fires of the last century were the toys of white and wealthy men, in the days when it was a privilege to be a fireman, and they paid handsome annual fees to be so hailed and put themselves on the path of the civic hero. It was at a black tie affair, a kind of Academy Awards ceremony, when the most courageous of the firefighters, and the speediest of the companies, were honored with the coveted prizes of masculinity. The rivalry among companies was intense. Their secret amusement, their thing, was arson. Sauce for the bored elite. How better to ensure that one's company be first on the scene? No homes. These men were not murderers, after all. Until after hours, no businesses. And why not, if one is going to burn, why not the business of a member of a rival company, whose home you were so lavishly, so recently, entertained in, as you'd entertained him? As you would continue to entertain each other, knowing all the while and accepting the rules of the game. In the smoky and sooty Utica of '50 and '51, two Italians lurked."

"Lurked? They were criminals?"

"They were Italians."

"Yes. Lurked. They belonged to nothing but themselves. John Marchisi, who arrived in 1815, calling himself a doctor; Alessandro Lucca in 1850. In 1865, the fateful third on Lucca's doorstep appears: Primo Cesso, distant forefather of Albert, with whom (as even I can see) our Albert shares only a name."

"Only?"

"Where does he get off with 'only'?"

"People change their minds."

"No they don't."

"Like Satan, they just do themselves deeper."

"Each in his own way, a very great man. Each a giant of will. Children of God's Satan? Men. Think of the three as Lucca, as I give you Lucca now, a man of rare physical force, an artist of clay images, peddling from his boat along the Erie Canal, daily between Utica and Rome. The boat, his home. Mrs. Lucca, an agoraphobe, confined day and night, cowering in the boat. The Luccas too poor to purchase a mule to tug them along their daily way. See him, the man-mule in harness, rope about his waist, over his shoulders and crossing his chest, tugging and peddling nine miles daily. Or see the three now as the gallant Marchisi, when he is twenty-four. 1813. Canada. Where he marries his child bride, a twelve-year-old, flat chested and erotic, with whom he shares a bed but does not make love, technically, until 1817. He, also, suffering in the isolation of virginity, but unlike the twelve-year-old: for his entire life, who makes his fortune by compounding what he was pleased to advertise as Dr. Marchisi's Italian Piles Ointment, and by concocting his Uterine Catholicon, which achieves international acclaim for the cure of female disorders: a mere salad dressing, his pharmaceutical competitors will sneer (not without foundation). Or see them all as Primo Cesso, on his Atlantic crossing learning but two words of English. In the beginning, Primo haunts with impunity the swampy and weedy land along the dung-studded towpath of the Erie, ignoring signs that declare City Property. No Trespassing. The thin man, the police called him, because they'd never seen thinner. This harmless foreigner, without friends and family, boarding free with Lucca in 1865, when the man-mule ·purchases Utica's only groggery on the canal, a shack of three rooms, a place of filth and violence, frequented mainly by the Erie Canallers, boatmen whose brutality is surpassed only by their bold lawlessness, who would come to fear, on the entire course of the canal, only one man: Alessandro Lucca of the twenty inch neck. In 1866, three more Cessos arrive and board with Lucca, free, in the third room. They do their business in the canal, where they bathe and wash their clothes. In '67, nine more Cessos: thirteen in a room, free, business in the canal, washing their clothes, bathing, without a word of complaint. Lucca builds an additional room, eight by eight, for his son and daughter. Mrs. Lucca cooks for the thirteen Cessos, who provide their own pasta, adequate for seven, lettuce adequate for six, bread adequate for five. Onward in wiry health. Cesso power. No charge for lodging. Thirteen Cessos, each earning six dollars per week in the brickyards, sixteen hours per day, Monday through Friday. Four on Saturday. Paying no rent because Alessandro Lucca cannot bear to ask a countryman in need. Alessandro, the anti-Satan. Thirteen swarming Cessos, keeping their appetite in reserve, haunting on weekends the swamp land. The authorities react. A policeman delivers a court order to vacate. Primo Cesso accepts the document. And then, he, Primo Cesso, by an act of will never before achieved, because nature does not call, nature is nowhere in the neighborhood, Primo drops his trousers, defecates magnificently, and wipes his behind with the document as he utters the two words that he'd learned on the Atlantic crossing: "Squatter's rights." By 1871, Primo had married Lucca's daughter, Lucca's son had married a Cesso, and Primo owned 1,000 running feet of so-called worthless land along the towpath. In 1872, Mrs. Lucca dies, and Alessandro gives the saloon to Primo."

"Gives?"

"Gives. In 1874, Lucca is dead. The public records show a gift. The son and daughter bury him. The gravestone bears one word: Lucca. No dates. The eldest son of Lucca's son, early in this century, legally changes the name after his father dies, and under this new name the blood of Alessandro Lucca hides. Many hidden Luccas have since left Utica. A few stayed. As we speak, one remains."

"What was the new name?"

"Lancaster."

"I don't know any Lancasters."

"That's a new one on me."

Alex says, "I would have thought they'd change it to Lucas." Big laughter.

Raymond says, "You look Italian as much as I do."

"Do you know this person? The last remaining Lancaster?"

"He is unknown to me."

"In our family, only one saying of Primo is known. 'I never took a vacation, because all you do is waste time.' This is a saying we say at the beach, in memory of our forefather."

Spina says, "Your endless family, Albert, owns half of Sylvan Beach and three quarters of this town."

"Three-quarters of the time I don't see three-quarters of the family."

Paternostra: "Albert won highest honors at Hamilton College. Forget the sins of the fathers."

"Primo bribed the police. With one hand he wiped, with the other he gave eight dollars. More than a week's salary for a policeman. Remember: The Cesso revenue was seventy-eight dollars per week, a great sum in those times, with almost no expenses, thanks to Lucca. Every week a different policeman collects. After four years of collecting, the city sells the swamp land to Primo for one dollar. Cesso the First had met with Marchisi, by then a pillar, a man of extensive choice properties, who'd supplied Utica's finest with sensitive ointments and liquids.

He, Marchisi, on behalf of Primo, arranges the secret meeting with the chief of police, whom he'd personally fitted for a truss, and who insists that the self-certified doctor attend the meeting. See him, Marchisi, as he eased the nether scourge of the firefighters, easing while stitching together the swaggering hints of those grateful arsonists, whose crimes were long known to the chief, whose job they funded. One week after this meeting Primo has his property, and into the world of Governor Cosby, Philip Schuyler, and Rutger Bleecker, Primo Cesso moves, the first Italian-American expression of nativist themes. The one original feature in this tale lies in the role played by Marchisi."

Raymond: "A mediator at this type of meeting is not an original role. He necessarily gets a little. Ask Joseph. Ask Muzzy."

"We have only remote knowledge."

"Marchisi took nothing in cash or favors of a personal sort."

"He took a favor of an impersonal sort?"

"He took something."

"Tell us what he took. Tell us now."

"Why does he have to lurk if he's a pillar?"

"Primo threatens to expose the police department," says Raymond, "they kill him right away, because he's nobody. This is what occurs in a realistic world. That's one point. The other is how do you know these intimate details of real people? Why does Lucca permit himself to be destroyed by the thin people? You were in Marchisi's bedroom? You know what went on in there for four years before he did the job on her?"

"If Marchisi is twenty-four in 1813," says Ayoub, "then he was born in 1789. The child of revolution."

"Yes. The new wisdom of the world. In sum, a born killer. Through all seasons, day and night, he wore a skullcap. To contain and preserve the native heat. This alone belongs to me. This, at the end of my long life, he died in 1885, is what I know. It is the lesson of democracy. You have your personal heat and I have mine. We are responsible to ourselves. When asked, toward the end, to what he attributed his robust health and long life, he replied: 'To my custom of eating always at home.' Never once did he accept invitations from the English, Dutch, and German stalwarts of the community. Not once. Nor did he ever invite them into his home. A short, stocky, and cheerful man who, when Mrs. Marchisi died in '78, cried continuously for almost twelve hours and gave himself an eye infection. He was eighty-eight when she died. 'She was so good-looking.' Over and over. 'She was so good-looking.' "

Raymond: "The four years of waiting built up a tremendous surplus. They did it in their eighties and he still had some left when she went. The personal heat that he poured into her, who he loved."

Spina: "Plus she was the basis of his fortune. Because that's what he must have done for four years. He's constantly examining her negative parts for four years and he comes up with the ointment and the Catholicism. His love child and his fortune in one or two sensitive spots."

"Yes and no. He was apprenticed to an apothecary at the age of fourteen in his native Turin. It was then, he claimed, that he compounded the Italian Piles Ointment, which he would deploy in Italy, France, Russia, and Canada, wherever he traveled, blown by the winds of democratic promise. In Italy, France, and Russia with his hero Napoleon Bonaparte. Marchisi had joined the French army in 1806. We imagine the hemorrhoids of soldiers who have to retain too long. To the magic of Marchisi's medicine, even the general himself attested."

"A kind of lubricant, right?"

"No."

"For the long Russian winter."

"I doubt it."

"Why? Kill two birds with one stone."

"The actual begins to knock at his door. The knocking becomes louder when he's captured by the British in Sicily, and is given a choice. Join the British army or forevermore live in this prison hole in Sicily."

"Go with the conservers of tradition, or keep your individuality in this hole."

"Obviously he joins."

"Upon which he is sent to Gibralter and then to Canada. 1811. His apothecary skills are valued. Even more so his fluency in the languages of Europe. A cosmopolite, who is given rank. He acquires the first skullcap in this period. Wears it only in periods of cold. Nondescript. Cheap. It is 1812."

"The Anglo-American conflict."

"Stationed at Fort George, near Kingston, when the fort is captured by the Americans."

"Who don't throw him down the hole."

"The point of the skullcap is he changes sides again. The politics of personal heat."

"A superb guess, Mr. Spina."

"I want to guess too, Robert. He now buys a top-of-the-line skullcap. A velvet one, for America, which he wears day and night forever. Am I wrong?"

"In effect, you are not wrong, Alex. He marries Catherine Forbis of Kingston in 1813, with the blessing of her parents, and then we enter the deeper dark. We have no evidence for the period 1813 to 1815. In 1815, he appears in Utica."

"She can pass now. She's developed up front."

"He's on the run with the twelve-year-old in the deep dark. Village to village, his perpetual hard-on leading the way. He keeps one step ahead of the scandal. The lynchers. Somebody threatens to cut his balls off."

"And why not, Raymond? He kept detailed, if virtually undecipherable records. The diaries are exhaustively quotidian. They bore us. What leaps out theatrically is the gap itself. 1813 to 1815. The gap needs filling."

"The period of the passage of fingers. The time of the tongue. According to you."

"That I never said."

"You said technically no love-making."

"Because he was a serious Catholic."

"Catholics get erections."

"Devout ones do not use contraception. He carried no means in his pharmacy. He refused to give advice in this area. It's in the diaries, gentlemen."

"What the hell is a revolutionary Catholic?"

"The answer, Professor, is John Marchisi. Their first child was not born until 1818. This is how we know of their technical chastity for four years. In Utica, his career is meteoric. He works for a certified doctor. He opens a pharmacy. He opens several pharmacies. He is Mr. Pharmacist. He opens the Drug Emporium, a kind of supermarket we would say. Perhaps America's first. He opens the City Gardens and Baths. Acquires numerous commercial and residential properties. He is constantly, constantly changing his residence. Thirteen different residences that we know of, twelve of these moves undertaken when his financial base is secured."

"Fort Marchisi."

"How many children did he have?"

"Seven."

"That explains the moves. He has to accommodate the expanding brood. The little goats need room."

"Seven who survived infancy. In addition to the six who did not."

"He was a true Catholic of the nineteenth century. Wives in childbirth and children in infancy. If you desired three for your old age, then you needed to have six. But the expanding brood does not explain. Eight of those moves occur in Catherine Marchisi's sixties, when John is in his seventies. There is much talk. John Marchisi, with his wealth and stature, had become, in his seventies, an itinerant inside the boundaries of the city he had lived in for fifty years. In the mansions of upper Genesee and Rutger Park, he was the topic. Someone finally asked. The question was posed, against all norms of civility. Why, so late in life, John? He is said to have responded: 'My parents were heedless of their health. Their diet was unbalanced. The medicines then were not good. They accepted many invitations to dine out and died before their time, in their early eighties. I am not late in my life, and you are wrong to think that I have just begun to behave in the fashion of the young and the worthless. I started to move in 1806.' And he was asked, 'What happened in 1806 that caused you to make your first move?' And he responded, 'I joined Napoleon and began to take the first steps in my long journey. I was moving to America. And now, sir, I will answer your question as to what I am doing in my so-called late years. This is my answer: I am moving to America. How do you like my new skullcap? The very highest grade of velvet.' "

Paternostra: " 'Velvet' is the word we use in certain circles to say that we are ahead when we gamble. How much you're winning is your velvet. I never gambled."

Ayoub: "A synonym for gain beyond expectation."

Paternostra: "Luck. Which I never depended on. Better to run the game, like a bank runs its mortgages. You get so much regardless. Tell me one thing, Mr. Tagliaferro. Lucca had a physical power that all feared, including those animals of the Erie Canal. Why does he let the skinny people walk all over him? You say he can't charge another Italian, but we charge each other all the time. We extract what is necessary, whenever necessary. We all do this in our own little ways. Extract. I don't accept your understanding of that point."

Cesso: "There are gaps in your story, Robert."

Spina: "Stories are not facts, so why argue with the man is my belief."

"You have all helped me to fill in the gaps, including you, Mr. Spina. Mr. Paternostra doesn't accept my understanding of Lucca's motive and I, myself, am dissatisfied. Therefore, he must give us a better one."

Paternostra: "He was weak."

Alex: "They smelled his weakness, like wolves who in pursuit of the herd go after the old, the infirm, and the young. They ate him alive."

Cesso: "He was good. They took advantage."

Spina: "He was stupid. They took advantage."

Raymond: "Some people like to be dominated."

Ayoub: "He gave and wanted nothing in return. In return, they gave nothing."

Robert: "Did they not give a son to his daughter? A daughter to the son?"

Raymond: "But he was letting them off long before the marriages."

Robert: "He gave extreme pain to the wretched canallers."

Raymond: "He doesn't let the canallers dominate his ass, so why the Cessos?"

Spina: "He made artistic images, he knew nothing."

Ayoub: "We're reduced to Albert's thesis. Pathetic!"

Alex: "He was good?"

Spina: "Define it. What is good? Not to charge those in so-called need? That's the welfare department's job, which they should exterminate that department. A person can't do that job."

Robert: "Why not?"

Spina: "You see where it led?"

Cesso: "Where did it lead, Sebastian?"

Spina: "It's obvious."

Cesso: "Where, Sebastian?"

Spina: "If you have to ask, you got problems, Albert. They took him for a ride."

Robert: "Yes. But nowhere is it indicated that he complained. He gave more. He gave the saloon. Two years before death, in great health, he gives the saloon to Primo Cesso. Then the fatal coronary. They in their minds were certainly taking advantage. But in his mind? It is precisely not obvious, Mr. Spina. This is a mystery. What was in his mind?"

Ayoub: "Nothing. The man had no inner life, where he could keep his secrets, where he could know himself, and nurse his fucking resentments!"

Alex: "Like a mother, giving suck to her child, to make it strong, so that eventually it grows up to—"

Paternostra: "Lash out without mercy!"

Cesso: "He was good, which I define as everything that's left over in Lucca when we subtract everything that you boys have said."

Raymond: "His humanity is so great he becomes inhuman, this wimp from heaven. Fuck good."

Robert: "Perhaps he did not feel, 'I am giving.' Perhaps he did not even have in his mind, 'I am giving without desire for return.' "

Spina: "Does the Pope know about the Saint of Utica? It made him feel good to do this. This is how he was paid. You can't deny it."

Ayoub: "I deny it. He had no inner life where he could treasure this pleasure. This is my thesis. He had no self."

Alex: "Satan gets himself an inner life and a self, and then look out! Lucca was an unfallen angel. Thoughtlessly, without reflection, he does good. That is the meaning of his nature."

Robert: "To exist nakedly, only in the act. The act akin to habit. The act beyond the actor's conscious examination, until the act is disrupted, and called to his attention. To do acts of goodness stupidly. Merely to do. Without harness. He was beyond comedy and tragedy. He was Lucca."

Ayoub: "You just converted stupid into an honorific term."

Alex: "What can you say about such a man?"

Paternostra: "This man walked around in a fog."

Raymond: "While the Cessos robbed him blind."

Spina. "Amen."

Ayoub: "He never put himself outside. He did not destroy himself."

Alex: "What can we say except he's nothing like me?"

Cesso: "Or anybody we know."

Alex: "What can we say except, Who is this mystery on earth?"

Robert: "Amen."

Alex stares hard at Robert, trying to make him flinch in acknowledgment of another story of Lucca that Robert had told him on the first night. Robert shows him nothing but a kindly smile. Between the two of them, something will be clarified before this night is out, though not in this room.

The Cesso clan requires no more commentary. The Cessos are a sizable fact of Utica's unwritten history, and Robert has given the men in Joe's cellar the originary myth of impervious will, Cesso inevitability, and they are satisfied. They know the Cessos. They know Albert well, but not as a Cesso, because he falls outside the myth. On the subject of Lucca, they had all urged each other on in unexpected collision with another impervious reality, and even Joseph, in his way, accepts the enigma of a stupid goodness, doing its work in the absence of reflective intelligence and sense of duty and, "therefore," as Ayoub would note in the epilogue of his book: "better than Christ, because truly natural, and unlike our own occasional acts of kindness, which are excretions of the will. He never cried out, Father, why hast thou forsaken me?"

But with Marchisi they are not finished. They want more story. Robert tells them that he can give additional narrative detail but cannot promise to fit it into narrative form. They tell him not to worry about the form. So he tells them about the arrival in Utica, in 1817, of the tomato, the year before Catherine Marchisi's first pregnancy. How Uticans did not believe that such things were worthy of being eaten, they called them "love apples," and raised them for ornament. Celery too they would not eat, in 1817, in Utica.

"But Marchisi was an Italian," says Raymond. "He knew the value of the tomato and the celery. He can now make a proper pasta sauce, but the sauce does not cure. He doesn't feel closer to Italy and he's still lost in the New World, looking for America."

Robert tells them of Marchisi's earliest memory of childhood, of being shaken like a rag doll, but not screaming, only the eyes, like two full moons, registering the event.

Cesso: "The father's violence. The beginning of the need to move constantly to America."

Paternostra: "This man is interesting. But if Albert is right, then he's no longer interesting."

Alex: "He becomes a reflex to authority."

Ayoub: "Etcetera."

Spina: "This is what you call a deep meaning in college. In other words, it's boring."

Then Robert says, "Like Lucca, he married a woman who didn't speak his language. They were two lone immigrant males, who didn't speak their wives' language. Think of it: each trapped in a native tongue unknown to the spouse and no third language, not for a long while, in common. Think of them together in this way, in private, each plunged in his own mood, trying to come to the surface. Bodies. Acts. No words. And Marchisi with the additional limitation: the self-imposed interdiction on consummation in the technical sense."

Ayoub: "Marchisi. Four years. Chained to the burning lake of his desire. Cloistered his entire life in desire for a New World life."

Spina: "They do everything except the main event. Obviously."

Raymond: "Which only makes the fire of what they can't do hotter. The guy's cock feels like it's going to explode. A tongue goes only so far, is my experience."

Alex: "He goes into his mind deeper. He becomes the specialist in the nether parts. Perfects the Italian Piles Ointment. Invents the Uterine Catholicon in Utica. Ut! Ut! In his misery, a gift to women everywhere. Chained to the burning lake, he became scientific. What choice did he have? Yearning is the mother of progress."

Ayoub: "In his loneness, he was loony."

Robert: "His sons died without issue, and the daughters married non-Italians. Marchisi lurks in God only knows how many other names."

Ayoub: "Loonely in me loneness."

Raymond: "Mr. America, John Marchisi. Mr. Isolation."

So caught up, on they go, forgetting to ask the question about Marchisi's original role in the Primo Cesso affair, when he, Marchisi, according to Robert, in a Lucca-like gesture, took nothing for himself.

Commotion above. They look. She descends, Heather Faxton.

Weeks later, Raymond tells Joseph: "She made me feel for a few seconds like a closeted heterosexual." Spina, a man of average height, will refer to her as a "very tall woman." "The structure on her," he would say. Cesso will say, "Light in the bones, even for a woman of her smallish height." He will say, "A little too thin for her own good. But they all are these days."

At the foot of the ladder, still several feet from the men, she gives the impression that she's plugged in. Literally. Ayoub will claim that he actually looked for the electrical cord that must have been attached to her. There will be strong disagreement as to whether the glow increased, or diminished, as she approached the table.

Alex, to himself, as she approaches: "We speak the same language, but we don't use it often, so far."

They freeze. Do not rise to greet her. She speaks: "On the sidewalk, as I was about to enter, a man said something curious, which I pass on for what it's worth. He said: 'This building is about to burn down.'"

———————

The mystery was how someone could possibly have gotten into John's constantly locked personal toilet to start this trivial fire, which brought four fire trucks to Pellettieri Ave and sent the cellar diners on their way, out to the sidewalk, with entreaties from all to Robert to return soon and tie up the loose ends. Raymond said, "Those three guys, they were the same and totally different at the same time." Robert replied, "Loose ends are good."

Now Alex and Robert are sitting in Robert's room, and Alex is saying, "I'm not concerned with the loose ends but with a massive contradiction known to me and you and nobody else. The story you gave me the other night about Alessandro doesn't square with what you said tonight. He refused to eat shit, you said. After they ate the intestines, they became enraged when he wouldn't lend them his handkerchief to wipe their bloody faces. He was tragic, you said. You yourself were seething as you told this story. You were vomiting anger."

"You, also, Alex. The astroturf. They eat each other's dogs on Mary Street. Fear creates love. *[Pause.]* We were narrating in the truth of our anger. Then something happened."

"What? You mean Heather?"

"Even now. Something is taking its course."

"Another forgery, which I recognize this time."

"Yes. Mr. Beckett."

"Another literary father?"

"Yes."

"You love these literary fathers?"

"Yes. *[Pause.]* Mainly."

"What is taking its course?"

"Something."

"You don't know, do you?"

"No."

"What do I do with the two pictures of Alessandro Lucca?"

"Pick the one that you prefer to live with. You who took me in when you had good reason not to."

[Pause.]

"They're all going to want to know about Marchisi's secret role in the Cesso negotiation, what went on behind closed doors in the police chief's office, when Marchisi took nothing for himself."

Robert grins broadly.

"In other words, how could you know?"

"In other words. Alex. To this point in all of human history, eighty-two billion have walked the earth. About six billion yet do. Seventy-six billion dead. Mostly unrecorded. Not even a name. Most of the surviving names can be attached to nothing. A little bunch of letters called a name, written somewhere. That's all. How many names in all of human history can you remember, not counting the living? If you wrote these names on paper, how many sheets would it take? Think of Rutger Bleecker. You know him now. An absent namer, looking to the village of Utica and the future, who said, Let the streets be named thus. In his final months, knowing that he was dying, and his young wife pregnant (the first two taken in childbirth), he stipulates the name of the unborn child. The thrill of creating, founding, naming! Like God and Adam in one, Rutger Bleecker in Albany, paring his fingernails. I look the other way. To the past. Say the names in stories, if you can, at great tables, and assign the names deeds. And then the names become local presences, who attend upon us still. Say Utica, and they come."

"God alone knows all the names and deeds and what goes with what."

"We do a little of God's work. On occasion. In our stories. 'Borne back ceaselessly into the past,' said Mr. Fitzgerald. With all due respect, beautiful but untrue. Unless we carry ourselves back to the past, and to the dead, who need us. The living and the dead. We require each other's presence."

"Who are you, Mr. Tagliaferro?"

"Alex, the uncanny Phoenician understood. In the freshness of the founding act, in the very candor of birth, he names it Utica, signifying, says an obscure philologist, 'like an old and stately father.' Does it not please you? I mean, metahistorically considered? You ask, Who *am* I? Me? Like America itself, upon discovery, I am old. A man made of old words. Other people's words. In a manner of speaking, I am a happy man. You, as you said at the bus station, are the wedding guest in Mr. Coleridge's poem, and I the ancient mariner. Murder, Mr. Guest, we feel on the pulse. Love is against the grain. Hard work."

"How many times has that been said?"

"Eighty-two billion."

[Pause.]

"In the livery of his nakedness."

"Alex?"

"A phrase that kept coming to me all night. How I keep seeing Alessandro Lucca."

"Follow the phrase."

"I'll see you in the morning, Robert."

"*Speriamo.*"

"What's that?"

"Italian. Of which I have little and you have none. *Speriamo.* We hope."

Da Capo

Daybreak. Robert dons his formal white shirt. Rolls sleeves up and over the elbows. Caroline's jeans. Alex's tie. Melvina's white watch cap. Looks in the mirror: the week-old stubble is acquiring character. Nods to the image in the mirror.

In the realty office, he'll leave behind three suitcases, the large ones filled with his notebooks. Carrying the fourth, a child's size, he's about to pass Alex's desk when he notices. Stops. Picks up and puts on Alex's sunglasses. Deposits a twenty-dollar bill in the ashtray. For the glasses. Because he cannot afford to pay for the tie and the jeans. Sits at desk: writes.

———————⊰•◦•⊱———————

The weather on his final day in Utica has again turned cold, the mercury reaching a record low, as he walks briskly, sockless in his loafers, mangy sport coat over the shoulder, approaching now the Greyhound terminal, where he sees a newspaper boy, a black boy, perhaps twelve years old, arranging his stack of papers when a strong gust blows them everywhere. The boy tries to retrieve the irretrievable. Robert gives him a twenty-dollar bill, then enters the terminal.

One week ago, exactly, virtually to the hour, he'd gone to the terminal in Manhattan with 200 in cash. Purchased a one-way ticket to Utica: forty-five dollars. Twenty to Alex. Twenty to the newspaper boy. Reserves three dollars and with what remains wants to purchase a one-way ticket west, as far west as he can go, he tells the ticket agent. The agent tells him that one hundred and twelve dollars will take him to Sioux City, Iowa.

Two days later, in Sioux City, he spends the three dollars on a coke and a peanut butter sandwich.

———————⊰•◦•⊱———————

At nine A.M., Alex descends to his first floor office and takes in the three suitcases, the twenty-dollar bill, but not the letter. Goes quickly to Robert's room: As if no one had been living there for a week. Except for the large water glass on the coffee table. Filmy. Picks up the glass and notices the residue of finely crushed sea shells and ash.

At the terminal, he cannot find Robert. Speaks to an agent, who remembers the man that Alex describes. How could he forget what he'd said?

The agent says, "Would you be Alex Lucas?"

"Yes," Alex says. "I would be."

"Your friend said, 'Tell Alex Lucas that I'm moving to America. Address unknown.' "

When he returns to Pellettieri Ave, he finds the letter:

Dear Alex,

You will feel the impulse to share a generous portion of your new-found wealth with Darryl and his mother. Give in.

Sincerely,

Robert Tagliaferro

P.S. I have yet to see them. Have you? The amber waves of grain. The purple mountain majesties, above the fruited plain.

Lament of an Escape Artist

The immigrant groundskeeper—father to a nostalgic writer, long fled—removes the Welcome to Utica signs, because nothing is left but a vast, lush meadow, enclosed by a nine-foot chain-link fence, with coils of razor wire rolling and gleaming along the top rail. The fragile father of the nostalgic writer is too old. Nevertheless, he maintains the meadow vigorously, trimming with fanatic care along the fence and among the broken grave stones, as he jokes saltily to himself, aloud, in his native tongue. Then, one day, he stops. Much questioned by the son (from afar, in letters), he responds with silence, this immigrant face, with no expression, nothing to express. The vast meadow reverts to what it was when the Indians, who knew better, and would not live here, called this valley Mohawk. The chain-links rust, give way, to be smothered in thorny underbrush. The garlicky groundskeeper disappears. Like obscene fingers, upright and galvanized, the posts alone endure: *contra naturam*. Utica was here.

Author's Note

I am much indebted to Ron Pytko, my Utica bibliographer, who answered questions and supplied many obscure books bearing on my subject. A hearty thank you also to John Sharpe of the Duke University Library, whose ease with ancient languages made a strong contribution to the writing of several passages.

The publication of this novel was generously supported by the National Italian American Foundation and its peerless president, Dr. Ken Ciongoli, and by David and Patricia Montalto, Duke and Duchess, Fragneto Monforte, who were my splendid co-hosts at the Accademia Montalto, Benevento, Italy.

Tagliaferro's East Utica

John St.

Bla

Lan

Rut

Rutger Park

Eagle St.

Genesee St.

Oneida St.

Parku